Ruslan sprinted up the lane, dodging around slower runners. From behind him came a sound like a thousand bulldozers at full throttle, ripping through buildings and grinding them up. He glanced over his shoulder. A tremendous wall of black water had swept onto the south side of the peninsula and another onto the north, both submerging not only buildings but also coconut palms. The two walls collided with a deafening thunderclap that dwarfed the grinding roar. White spray erupted hundreds of feet high.

—From THE KILLING SEA

ALSO BY
RICHARD LEWIS

The Demon Queen

The Flame Tree

THE KILLING SEA

RICHARD LEWIS

Simon Pulse
New York   London   Toronto   Sydney

SIMON PULSE
An imprint of Simon & Schuster Children's Publishing Division
1230 Avenue of the Americas, New York, NY 10020
Copyright © 2006 by Richard Lewis
All rights reserved, including the right of reproduction
in whole or in part in any form.
SIMON PULSE and colophon are registered trademarks
of Simon & Schuster, Inc.
Also available in a Simon & Schuster Books for Young Readers
hardcover edition.
Designed by Christopher Grassi
The text of this book was set in Sabon.
Manufactured in the United States of America
First Simon Pulse edition April 2008
2 4 6 8 10 9 7 5 3 1
The Library of Congress has cataloged
the hardcover edition as follows:
Lewis, Richard, 1949–
The killing sea / Richard Lewis.—1st ed.
p. cm.
Summary: In the aftermath of the 2004 tsunami in Sumatra, two teenagers, American Sarah and Acehnese Ruslan, meet and continue together their arduous climb inland, where Ruslan hopes to find his father and Sarah seeks a doctor for her brother.
ISBN-13: 978-1-4169-1165-4 (hc)
ISBN-10: 1-4169-1165-0 (hc)
[1. Survival—Fiction. 2. Indian Ocean Tsunami, 2004—Fiction.
3. Tsunamis—Fiction. 4. Brothers and sisters—Fiction.
5. Americans—Indonesia—Fiction. 6. Sumatra (Indonesia)—Fiction.]
I. Title.
PZ7.L5877Kil 2007
[Fic]—dc22
2006001050
ISBN-13: 978-1-4169-5372-2 (pbk)
ISBN-10: 1-4169-5372-8 (pbk)

For Noni

Acknowledgments

Our rebuilding team in tsunami-ravaged Aceh had to start somewhere. We distributed symbolic sacks containing a shovel, a hammer, a saw, and a box of nails to devastated families picking through the rubble of their homes. The first family we approached had nothing left except the coconuts on their palms. One of the men climbed a palm and cut down several young coconuts, which he offered us. We were thirsty and gratefully accepted. Theirs was the greater offering, for they gave from what little they had. I would like to acknowledge that family, and the many other Acehnese I met, gracious and hospitable and persevering even as they grieved. They made my stint as a volunteer aide worker one of the best things I've ever done, and to them I say *teurimeng geunaseh*.

I'm grateful to Samaritan's Purse, who took me in and put me to work.

Thanks to my agent Scott Miller, who encouraged me to write this story, and to my editor David Gale, who trusted me to do so.

Kristie Cutter, Susan Henderson, and Hannah Holborn read an early draft of the novel and made invaluable suggestions. Ramesh Avadhani stepped in at a crucial time and lent his wise and encouraging voice. I am grateful to Judith Beck, who provided advice as both doctor and writer. I thank as well the online writing community of Zoetrope.com and the colleagues there who read and commented on various excerpts.

Chapter 1

The nightmare again. The water rushed in from nowhere, from everywhere, swallowing him in an instant. He couldn't breathe. Couldn't find a way out. He was going to die—

Ruslan woke with a gasp. His heart thumped. He swung out of bed to stand in front of the second-story window, taking deep breaths of the cool night air. In the distance, beyond the shacks and houses of Ujung Karang, moonlight glittered on the sea. He knew he wouldn't be able to fall asleep again, so he sat down at his desk, turned on the light, and opened his sketch pad.

Four years ago, when he was twelve, he'd had nightmares of a monster. He'd drawn its picture, its scaly body and fanged head and barbed tail, and then ripped the monster in half. The monster never bothered his sleep again.

Perhaps if he could draw the drowning nightmare, he could banish it as well.

But he didn't know how to draw it. He often swam in the rivers and played in the ocean waves, but this drowning water was different. He didn't know its shape or form. All he knew was its color.

Black.

After the morning's only customer paid his bill and left the waterfront café, Ruslan sat down at a rickety plywood table shaded by one of the palm trees. He cradled his head on his outstretched arm. His huge yawn nearly dislocated his jaw.

Why was he having such awful nightmares? Perhaps it was the sermon at the mosque the other Friday. The preacher had warned of the coming flood of God's judgment for liars and sinners. Was it a sin to drive his father's motor scooter without a license? Ruslan didn't think so. One could sin against God, sure, but how could one sin against the police?

A breeze ruffled the harbor's water, and the sun twinkled off its surface. Tiny waves lapped against the shore's breakwater. A big tug tied to the pier released its ropes and gunned its diesel, smoke belching from its stack. Its propeller churned the low tide, stirring up black sand and muck into a dark boil. Ruslan frowned, an uneasy feeling pricking him, but the water quickly cleared to its usual murky green. He yawned again. The breeze felt good on his face. His eyes grew heavy. He'd have a quick nap, just a minute's snooze—

"Excuse me. Ah, *maaf permisi*."

Ruslan's eyes flew open. He jerked upright, staring dumbfounded at the Western family standing before him. Father, mother, daughter, and son, their long noses red from the sun. Even the half-grown orange cat rubbing against the boy's ankle seemed foreign. Had they emerged from out of his sleep?

The big white man held an English-Indonesian dictionary in his hand. He flipped through pages with oil-smudged fingers and found what he was looking for. "*Mesin rusak*," he said. Broken engine. He nodded over his shoulder at a gleaming white sailboat that had just anchored off the jetty. He flipped more pages. "*Bengkel*." Mechanic's garage.

Ruslan stood. "I speak English." As well he should. Ever since he was four, he'd been tutored privately in English at his father's insistence.

"You can? Great. One of the fishermen there

pointed to you, said your father's a mechanic. At least that's what I thought he said."

Ruslan nodded. "My father is Yusuf the mechanic." Ruslan usually spent most of his free time helping his father in the garage, but he had wanted to earn some money to buy a new set of paintbrushes. A friend had gotten him this part-time job at the café, afternoons after school and all day during Sundays and national holidays, such as today.

The girl stepped forward and squinted at the café's small display fridge. She and her mother wore long wrinkled dresses, and her mother a head scarf, but the girl's blond hair glowed in the sunlight, her scarf wadded up in her hand. She had the bluest eyes Ruslan had ever seen. The *only* blue eyes he'd ever seen, at least in real life and not on TV. "Hey," she said, "they have cold Cokes right here."

"Well, I'll be a soda pop," the father said. "Wonder if they have cold beer."

"I'm sorry, no," Ruslan said. "We are a Muslim province. We don't sell alcohol."

"I know. Just fantasizing. Can we have four Cokes?"

As Ruslan got out the drinks, a dozen kids gathered to gawk at the Westerners. Meulaboh, a small harbor town, didn't get nearly as many foreign visitors as the big city of Banda Aceh, with its grand mosques and golden beaches. Several other people sauntered down the breakwater to also have a look at the strangers.

The mother whispered to the girl, "Put on your scarf."

"This stupid dress is enough. I'm drowning in sweat."

"It's the local custom."

"But I'm not a local, am I? If they get offended, it's their problem, not mine."

"Put on your scarf."

"Soooo barbaric."

"Sarah. Respect their culture."

"I put on my scarf at Banda Aceh. It's *their* turn to respect *my* culture."

"If you don't put on your scarf, you go back to the boat."

The daughter glared at her mother, who calmly returned the glare with a level gaze. Ruslan, intently watching this drama out of the corner of his eye, nearly dropped one of the Coke cans as he put them on the table. He couldn't imagine any teenage girl in Meulaboh defying her mother like this. "Fine," the girl snapped, and stalked back toward the jetty, where an inflatable dinghy was tied up to one of the bollards. She paused and said over her shoulder, "You don't have to love me, Mom, but you should at least respect me as much as you do these total strangers."

"Whoa," the freckle-faced boy said. "Sarah's sure in a bad mood."

The mother gave the father an exasperated look, quickly tilting her head at the girl, telling the father to have a word with her. He grabbed a Coke off the table and strode after the girl. Catching up to her, he handed her the soda and spoke with her. She listened, rolling the icy can around her frowning, sweaty face. She shook her head. "I'm not going to wear a scarf just to keep Mom from being embarrassed," she said loudly. Ruslan was sure she meant for her mother to overhear. "That's so hypocritical."

Her father said something that Ruslan didn't fully catch, something about Christmas and family. The girl firmly shook her head. The father gave the mother a big shrug that said *I tried* and took his daughter out to the boat in the dinghy.

When he returned, he said to his wife, "Our darling daughter's hardly full of Christmas cheer, is she?"

"You shouldn't have let her have the Coke. Coddling her when she's like this doesn't help."

"We'll give her cat food for lunch."

"Steve. That's not funny."

"Just trying to lighten things up. 'Tis the season to be jolly, after all." He paid for the drinks and asked Ruslan, "Where can we find your father?"

The narrow peninsula of Ujung Karang, sticking out of Meulaboh like a tail, was a maze of streets and lanes where thousands of people lived. Ruslan's house and his father's attached garage were at the base of the peninsula, near the big stadium. Haji Kamarudin, a pensioner with gray hair bristling out from underneath his white skullcap, pushed through the crowd and told Ruslan he'd be honored to show the guests the way. He shook hands with the father, mother, and boy, welcoming them to Meulaboh. Ruslan knew the Haji would first detour to his own house, where he'd offer the guests coffee and cakes. He was a grand old man who always had a kind word for everyone and was curious about everything.

"Come on, Surf Cat," the boy called out. The cat trotted off with the humans, tail high in the air.

An hour later the Westerners and the cat reappeared with Ruslan's father Yusuf, who was wearing his mechanic's gray overalls and carrying his satchel of tools. The boy kicked a scuffed soccer ball back and forth with several of the local kids. He looked to be eight or so, and his body hadn't yet grown to match his big, clumsy feet.

Yusuf put a skinny arm around Ruslan. "My son," he said. Yusuf had worked with Exxon in the northern oil fields for four years after the death of Ruslan's mother, and he spoke reasonable English. "No good mechanic, very good artist. He make your picture, okay?"

"Bapa," Ruslan muttered, feeling heat flood his cheeks, although he was pleased. Many fathers would have scolded their sons for such a worthless talent that didn't put rice on the table, but his father was proud of him. He planned to send Ruslan to an arts college in Jakarta.

The group headed for the jetty. "Oh, man," the boy said. "Now we gotta go back to Sarah. If she's still in her stinky mood, can we send her to shore?"

Ruslan wished they would. Those blue eyes. He wanted to study them some more. Politely, of course. Could he capture that color on canvas, show how light filled the blue?

Yusuf fixed the engine, and the sailboat left that afternoon. Ruslan stood under the palms and watched as it motored out to sea. A rush of customers came in, demanding his attention, and when he next looked, the boat was gone, almost as if it had been swallowed up by the deep. Ruslan pondered the ocean, silvered by the late afternoon light.

Although there wasn't a storm cloud on the horizon, the ocean's cheerfulness had turned moody, even menacing. In his imagination the silver water slowly blackened—

"Get back to work," his boss yelled at him.

The girl's blue eyes wouldn't leave him alone. That night he ate dinner by himself, as his father was busy doing another emergency repair on a truck. After dinner he went to his bedroom and got out his pad and pencil.

A few months ago one of the town's leading clerics had seen him sketching the face of an old woman and had ripped up the sketch. The making of images was forbidden, the cleric said, as that led to idolatry. For the first time in his life, Ruslan knew that a cleric could be wrong, and his world had cracked a little. He didn't dare sketch in public anymore, but in private he drew anything he wanted. Like the face of this Western girl, drawn from his memory. Using his pastel chalk, he touched the eyes with blue—not the right blue, he needed oil paints for that—and put just a hint of red to her lips, smudging the chalk with a wetted finger. He taped the sketch next to the poster of Siti Nurhaliza, the teenage Malaysian pop star he had a crush on. He contemplated both poster and sketch, trying to decide which girl was prettier.

Not that it mattered. Siti lived in a different world, and as for the Western girl, he'd never see her again in his life.

His father knocked on his door. He'd showered and had changed out of his gray overalls into a sarong. "Is everything okay?"

"Why?"

"You look tired. How are things at the coffee shop?"

"I know one thing now, Bapa. I don't want to work for other people. I want to be my own boss, have people work for me."

"It's good to have a job first, though," his father responded. "That way when you're a boss you'll know what it's like to be an employee."

Ruslan hesitated. "Bapa, last week I borrowed your motor scooter without asking. I'm sorry."

His father seemed startled. Then he laughed. "Did you borrow my helmet, too?"

"Yes."

"Good. Always wear a helmet. Listen, I'm going to be up early before dawn prayers to go work on the Pertamina oil tanker. I'll be home very late."

Before Ruslan went to bed, he gazed out the window. In the outer harbor the oil tanker was placidly at anchor. The big ship cast a moon shadow on the water. The single cloud in the sky fell across the moon, and the sea darkened, obscuring the tanker. A shivery feeling raced from Ruslan's neck down to his arms. Then the cloud moved off, the light returned, and the ship reappeared in the night's sparkling sea.

Chapter 2

Sarah was asleep in her forward cabin, dreaming she was back home celebrating her sixteenth birthday with friends in a deliciously cold, air-conditioned mall, when a pounding on the door woke her. It was already morning, with a warm blue sky pressing against the porthole's glass. Despite the cabin's whirring fan, sweat filmed her skin.

Another bang on the door. It was her brother, Peter. "Sarah, Sarah, wake up."

"Shut up! Go away!"

"Surf Cat's climbed up the mast and won't come down."

Sarah groaned and put her pillow over her head.

Why, oh why, had she let her dad talk her into this crazy idea for a family vacation? So far the chartered sailboat cruise from Malaysia to Bali had hardly been the grand adventure he had promised. All she'd done was stew in the heat and squabble with her brother and fight with her mother about everything, from the water rationing to the use of the satellite phone to call her friends. And then, to top it all off, yesterday morning's big blowup about the stupid head scarf. On Christmas Day, no less, spent in some grotty, filthy town because of a broken engine. She and her mom still weren't speaking to each other.

Peter pounded on the door again. "Something's wrong. I don't know what, but Surf Cat's real scared."

Surf Cat was Peter's new pet, a half-grown kitten he'd rescued from a gutter at the Malaysia marina where they'd started the trip. Sarah lifted her pillow. From high above she could hear Surf Cat's agitated meowing. This wasn't the cat's usual begging for food or a rub. She glanced out the porthole. They'd already anchored here the other day, before the engine had broken, necessitating the detour. The bay's pastel water, the empty golden beach, and the hilly green jungle looked the same. The full-moon tide had washed away part of the sand castle she and her brother had built in the shade of an overhanging tree. Building a sandcastle for entertainment! If only her friends could have seen her.

Meow, meow, meow. God, that cat sure had big lungs.

Sarah pulled on a T-shirt over the black bikini bottoms she'd slept in and opened the door to Peter's scrawny, worried face.

"You are so annoying," she said, "that if a T. rex ate you, it would have indigestion for a week."

"You got to help me get Surf Cat down."

"Can I use the bathroom first?"

"It's called a head."

"It's still a bathroom."

"But Surf Cat—"

"Shut. Up. Go try a can of tuna."

In the tiny bathroom she washed her face and brushed her teeth. She studied her nails. They needed a manicure. New polish, too. She'd do that later. The day's big event. Give her something to look forward to.

She exited the bathroom. The stupid cat was still meowing. She sidled through the *Dreamcatcher*'s cramped saloon and galley. The door to the master cabin was partially open, and she could see her mom and dad sprawled on the bed, sound asleep. After they had left the town's harbor, her parents had decided to postpone Christmas dinner for a day, but they'd gotten into the Christmas wine. They rarely drank more than a glass or two, but they'd polished off a bottle on the sunset sail back to the island, and then another bottle after they had anchored, followed by a cognac nightcap.

Up on deck Peter held up an open can of tuna fish, trying to tempt Surf Cat down from the mast. The orange kitten squatted precariously on one of the upper rungs, mewing nonstop. How on earth had he managed to climb so high?

"Come on, Surf Cat, this is real tuna. Human tuna." Peter tossed a chunk up into the air. "Yum, yum. Come on down. You can have the whole can."

Surf Cat ignored the offering and clawed up another rung, almost losing his footing.

Sarah looked uneasily around her at the sea and the island. Tiger Island, it was called. The guidebook said there was still a small herd of wild Sumatran elephants living in the jungle, but it reassured readers that a Dutch hunter had killed the last remaining tiger seventy years ago. How could anybody know for sure, though? Maybe Surf Cat had spotted one. Maybe a tiger was eyeing Sarah's tasty, sun-toasted flesh from behind the dense wall of jungle, which seemed just a hop, skip, and a pounce away. Could tigers swim?

"I guess I'll have to climb up and get you," Peter announced to Surf Cat. He slipped into his sneakers and began to climb the metal rungs.

A loud trumpeting broke the jungle's morning quiet. Sarah spun and caught sight of two adult elephants and a juvenile running up a ravine on their stumpy legs. Monkeys began screeching, racing through treetops to higher ground. Across the bay, hundreds of birds exploded out of the jungle. All kinds of birds, small black swallows, big white storky ones, green parrots, all squawking and chirping and cawing.

The hoarse voice of Sarah's father rose out of the master cabin's open hatch. "Good God, who's stirred up the zoo?"

For a moment everything seemed to quiet down. Even Surf Cat stopped meowing.

Then there came a dull but powerful thud, which Sarah not only heard but also felt in her bones, as though a primal sound had risen from a deep place in the earth. The bay's placid water erupted in shivering, swirling patterns. The clear depths turned instantly cloudy. A tremendous force slammed into the sailboat's hull. The *Dreamcatcher* shuddered violently, rocking with a hard jerk on its anchor chain. The dinghy tied off to the side broke its line with a whip-snap. Sarah went sprawling onto the deck. Peter, reaching out a hand for Surf Cat, twirled around the mast and nearly fell before catching hold of a rung again. Surf Cat managed to hang on with his claws.

Sarah's father rocketed out of the hatch, wearing only his boxers. "What the hell?" he said, looking around him. He glanced up at the mast. "Peter! Get down from there!"

Peter climbed down, Surf Cat cradled in one arm.

Sarah's mother poked her head up from the hatch. Her hair was a complete mess, but her bleary eyes were clearing quickly. "What's all the commotion?"

The boat shuddered with another jolt. Across the bay, the top half of a steep cliff broke away and tumbled in a cloud of dust. Boulders rolled off a ridge and plowed into the lower jungle.

"I'll be a Richter," Sarah's father said in awe. "It's an earthquake, a big one. I think we'd better get out of here."

Sarah's mouth went dry. Her heart kicked against her ribs. But they were safe, weren't they? After all, there was no ground underneath to crack open, and there was nothing to fall down on top of them.

"Hey, the dinghy's loose," Peter said, pointing to it as it swiftly drifted away.

Sarah's father dove into the water and swam after the inflatable with long, urgent strokes. He had to row hard to get back to the *Dreamcatcher*, putting his back into it, digging deep with the oar paddles. "That's one hell of a current," he said as he tied the dinghy off to the stern. "Let's get going."

In the cockpit he turned the ignition switch. From below came a horrible whirring sound. The engine wouldn't catch. He crawled into the engine room with a flashlight as Sarah watched from the hatchway, biting her lip hard. *Hurry, hurry, hurry.*

"Starter's broken off its mounting," he said. "We'll have to sail out."

From up top came Peter's excited cry. "Hey, the reef's drying up! There's fish flopping around!"

Sarah's father jerked his head, banging it against a deck beam. He roared, "Betty, get the anchor up. Sarah, go help your mother."

Peter was already up on the bow helping their mother, who was still in her nightie. The anchor winch's electric motor whined as it hoisted the clanking chain. Sarah untied the mainsail cover with trembling fingers. Something was very, very wrong. Behind them live coral that yesterday had been underwater even during low tide now rose out of the surface, anemones and soft grasses drooped and wilted. A school of minnows flopped around one brain coral head like a silvery cloud.

Sarah's father hoisted the sail. He always remained calm in an emergency, and his actions were smooth and deliberate, but Sarah had never seen his jaw so rigid. A blood vessel pulsed in his neck. The sail caught the slight offshore breeze, and the *Dreamcatcher* began to inch forward toward the open sea.

Hurry, hurry, hurry.

Coral heads appeared out of the water all around them. Sarah's father had anchored the boat in the good holding ground of a deep sandy hole. Now the bowl of water was rapidly draining through crevasses in the reef. The *Dreamcatcher* was trapped.

Chapter 3

In the garage below Ruslan's bedroom, the Ford's temperamental engine banged and chugged to life. Ruslan opened an eye and peeked at the window. Stars still twinkled in the predawn sky. The Ford coughed once or twice more before settling down to a hum. The old car was his father's favorite. "Keeps me on my toes," he always said. Ruslan yawned into his pillow, wondering why his father was taking his car and not his scooter the short distance to the oil terminal.

But that curiosity vanished when he realized that for the first time in a week he hadn't had his drowning nightmare. He was sated with sleep. It felt delicious. No, more than delicious. He felt like a conqueror, full of a conqueror's courage. Today nothing would be impossible for him.

He glanced at the sketch of the Western girl taped to his bedroom wall, her features barely visible in the glow of the streetlamp outside his window. Too bad he hadn't been like this yesterday. She would have noticed him then for sure, a strong and handsome hero who had the courage and strength to rescue her from all dangers.

Well, there were other girls to impress. Tjut Sari, for example, a flashing-eyed beauty who worked at the photocopy shop. Today he'd saunter in with some document to copy. He'd hand it to her. "Two copies, please," he'd say in his assured and commanding voice, and she would look at him with startled wonder.

His reverie was broken as mosque speakers all over town burst to life, summoning the faithful to dawn prayers. After washing, he prayed in the second-floor prayer room. Then, with the clear dawn sky filling with blue, he hurried downstairs and across the lane to buy several hot banana fritters from Ibu Ramly's stand. Of all the neighborhood ibus, the mothers and grandmothers, she was his favorite. The burner roared, fritters sizzling in the wok of hot oil.

"Such a handsome boy you're turning out to be,"

Ibu Ramly said, handing him two extra-large fritters wrapped in newspaper. "Your mother would be proud."

Ibu Ramly had grown up in the same hill village of Ie Mameh as Ruslan's mother. Ruslan had been three when his mother was killed during a firefight between jungle rebels and the military. He remembered nothing of her, and his father rarely spoke of her.

He went up to his bedroom to change his sarong for a pair of jeans to wear to work, but he didn't put on his shirt. He munched his warm fritters, thinking of the Western girl's mother and the fight they'd had. Western girls were clearly different from Acehnese girls, but were Western mothers different from Acehnese mothers? He didn't think so. Mothers were mothers. But then again, how would he know? He hadn't had one.

He fell onto his back on the bed, thinking. How different would his life be now if his mother hadn't been killed? How different would *he* be as a person if he'd had a mother as well as a father?

A curious ache that he'd never felt before stole into his heart.

And then he fell asleep again.

It seemed only a moment later that a tremendous shaking of his bed jerked him back to consciousness.

His first crazy thought was that he was late for work and that his angry boss was waking him. But no one was in the room.

His bed bounced. His wardrobe skittered across the floor. The whole house shook and rattled. One large pane of his window shattered.

Neighbors screamed, some shouting in incoherent fright, others bellowing out, *"Allahu Akbar!"*

The bed was really bouncing now. Ruslan jumped out of the broken window into the small side yard. The ground rolled underneath him. He couldn't keep his balance and had to crouch on all fours. Tiles fell from the house. One nearly hit his head, smashing to bits beside his feet. In the garage a tool cabinet toppled onto the motor scooter, smashing it to the floor. The air itself seemed to shudder and roar. Nothing in his vision remained stable, everything that should have been level and steady bounced and wavered. He closed his eyes to fend off nausea. Over the rattle and cracking Ruslan could hear his neighbor Ibu Ramly reciting Qur'an verses to soothe her frightened five-year-old boy.

At last the earth calmed, with only minor hiccups. Ruslan cautiously stood. Apart from several shattered windows and a few fallen roof tiles, the house looked okay, but all he could think about was his father, out on the oil tanker. Once before, a severed fuel hose had burst into flame, killing a handful of sailors. As Ruslan ran to the waterfront, he noticed that the shanties and houses on Ujung Karang had ridden out the earthquake with little damage. People milled around in shock at the powerful quake, grateful for their survival. Many began streaming to the mosque to pray, several women putting on their white robes as they hurried.

The Pertamina tanker was high on the water, its fuel already pumped to storage tanks on shore. Men moved around on the ship's deck.

The café owner saw Ruslan on the jetty and put him to immediate work, even though he was shirtless and shoeless. Excited customers packed the café—nothing like an earthquake to get people drinking coffee and smoking cigarettes, quacking to one another like ducks about the morning's moving experience.

One of the customers perked his head up and pointed to the ocean. "Hey, shouldn't the tide be *rising*?"

The tide not only dropped, it rushed out to sea, drying out the fringing coral and exposing the mucky bottom beyond for hundreds of yards. People flocked down to the seawall to watch. Many gleefully chased stranded fish. A grinning man held up a red snapper to his wife. "We'll eat well for free tonight!" he said, laughing.

Ruslan slopped a glass of coffee in front of the wrong man. Ignoring the boss's annoyed shout, he stared at the distant sea.

Out in the harbor the tanker's anchor lifted clear of the water as billows of smoke poured from its exhaust stack. Black water roiled off the stern, the propeller churning up sand from the seafloor as the ship made an ungainly turn toward the horizon.

Ruslan slipped away from the café and the curious onlookers. He began to run, not knowing exactly why, but instinct making him head away from the sea. His bare feet hurt, so he stopped at the house for a pair of sandals and snatched a yellow shirt from the front table as well.

He almost overlooked the letter on the table that he had already missed seeing once that morning. It was addressed to him in his father's handwriting. He stuffed the envelope into the shirt pocket.

And in the distance, along the seafront of Ujung Karang, screams rose from a hundred, a thousand, mouths.

Chapter 4

The water around the trapped *Dreamcatcher* continued to drain. Sarah's father grabbed the binoculars from the cockpit and aimed them out to sea. He was still focusing the knob when the *Dreamcatcher*'s keel touched bottom. The sailboat tilted, throwing him off balance and knocking him against the railing. The binoculars flew out of his hand and over the side.

"We'd better get off the boat. Everybody, pack a bottle of water. And put on your shoes." He said this as casually as if suggesting a picnic, but his hands were bunched into fists.

Sarah snatched her sandals from the cockpit box and crammed them on. Her father slipped into his loafers. Sarah's mother was below in the slanted galley, getting out the bottled water from the storage bin.

Peter, already wearing his sneakers, pointed seaward. "Look!"

At the mouth of the bay a wave was rolling in, no bigger than a normal beach wave. But beyond it the horizon was no longer flat and level against the sky. The ocean had risen into a wobbling cliff of water, sunlight glinting off the towering face.

"Betty!" Sarah's father roared. "Forget the bottles! Get the hell out! Everybody, off, off! Run for the hill!"

Sarah's mother raced up the companionway and took in the nightmare scene on the horizon with one quick look. She grabbed Peter by the arms and swung him off the stern of the boat, where the water had already dried out to damp sand.

"Surf Cat!" Peter cried. "Let me get Surf Cat!"

The cat hurtled past Peter and streaked across the dried reef toward the jungle.

Sarah and her parents jumped off the boat. The four of them sprinted toward the nearest spit of beach. Sarah came to an angled slope of coral that should have been underwater. The coral crunched under her sandals, slowing her down. Her father's hand pushed her. "Faster!"

Behind her she could hear a hiss of water rushing into the bay. From the exposed reef rose the familiar salty scent of low-tide wading pools, now mixed with a stink that smelled like sulfur. Several yards in front of her, the reef cracked open between two staghorn corals, and steaming green water erupted in a head-high geyser. She yelped and veered, which turned her at an angle so that she saw what happened next. The reef in front of her father split open and his leading leg plunged into the crack. The bone broke with an audible snap as he fell forward, his hand accidentally catching Peter on the ankles. Peter went tumbling as well.

The water from the first wave growled and gurgled onto the outer coral beds.

As Peter got to his feet, Sarah helped her mother pull her father out of the hole. His leg bent at a horrible angle midway between his knee and ankle.

The onrushing water swirled around the sailboat, spilling over its lower side. Sarah had no name for what was just outside the bay—it wasn't really a wave, but an uplifted chunk of dark water bigger than a city block. It loomed higher and higher over the mouth of the bay, tall enough to block out the morning sun and cast a shadow that raced over the shoreline.

"It's no good," Sarah's father said. "You guys get going."

Sarah's mother put an arm under his. Sarah did the same on his other side, but her mother pushed her arm away and said, "Take Peter. Run!"

"The highest ground," her father said, grunting between clenched teeth. His tanned face had gone sallow.

"No," Sarah said. She was dizzy with fear, but she had to help her dad.

Her mother slapped her on the cheek. Hard. Through her smarting tears, Sarah could see the implacable coldness of her mother's face. "You will obey me. Take Peter and run. Now!"

Sarah snatched Peter's hand. He resisted at first, crying incoherently. She gave him a vicious yank. They ran. She looked back once, when they reached the beach, and saw her mother helping her father hobble across the coral. Foamy water surged up around their waists, and they began to swim with its flow.

Sarah and Peter plunged through the wall of jungle. A vine's nasty needles tore the skin of her arms, but she felt no pain. Once behind the initial screen of vines and drooping branches, the jungle stretched spaciously uphill, with enormous trees scattered about like pillars supporting the high canopy. She ran up the steep slope, several times falling to her hands and knees. The ground was slippery with a thick layer of decaying leaves and mulch. With her longer arms and legs, she sometimes had to pull or push Peter along. Her heart pounded so hard she became afraid it would literally burst. Sweat poured off her.

How high were they? Were they safe? She paused, her chest heaving as she tried to catch her breath, and looked down the hill. Fifty feet below her, a tide of frothy brown water rose up the slope with hardly any noise. She seized Peter's arm and scrambled higher. The water caught up to them and floated them off the ground with a surprisingly tender touch. They soared on the surface of the upwelling, up through the trees, until Sarah's shoulder finally smashed into a branch. She clung to the branch in a daze. The water rose a few feet higher and then stopped. Sarah swung onto the branch and tucked herself against the main trunk. Peter's head bobbed among the drowned branches of the outer canopy. He swam toward Sarah as the water began to recede, slowly at first, and then with increasing speed, sucking him down with it.

"Swim harder!" Sarah shouted at him.

He put his head down into the mucky water and stroked furiously. She stretched out on the branch and reached out a hand. He grabbed it just as the water gurgled away from him, leaving her holding on to his dangling weight. She tried to haul him up onto the branch beside her, but his wet hand slipped away from hers and he fell back into the draining water five feet below. He looked up at her, his brown eyes wide with fright and shock.

"Grab something," Sarah shouted. "Anything!"

He managed to clutch a sapling, but the increasing violence of the receding water ripped it out by the roots. A growing whirlpool carried him down and out of her sight. Now the water had a voice, a full-throated roar filled with the grinding of stone and wood. Lower on the hill Sarah could see big trees toppling with great swishes of their branches as the earth was scoured away from beneath them.

She had no thoughts, only the sounds and the images, as if her mind were a video camera recording everything. No fear or pain or anguish. Just the detached certainty that her father and mother and brother were dead and she was still alive, being bitten all over her dirty, scraped-up body by a swarm of red ants.

Chapter 5

Ruslan rushed out of the house, his unbuttoned yellow shirt flapping, and abruptly halted on the front steps.

Far down the lane, men, women, and children shrieked as they ran in front of a surge of blackish brown water clogged with chunks of wood and plastic garbage. Several people gunned up the narrow track on motorbikes. A young man took a running jump onto the empty back of a scooter driven by a woman, sending both of them sprawling to the asphalt.

But what had frozen Ruslan on the porch was what he saw beyond the point of Ujung Karang. On all three sides of the peninsula, the whole ocean had lifted up and was racing landward. The sea was so tall that its face was visible above the houses and trees. From its top edge rose a churning white mist. One of the thirty-foot fishing boats got caught up in the frothing lip, which sent the vessel tumbling down the face.

The color of this sea was black.

That broke his trance. Ruslan sprinted up the lane, dodging around slower runners. From behind him came a sound like a thousand bulldozers at full throttle, ripping through buildings and grinding them up. He glanced over his shoulder. A tremendous wall of black water had swept onto the south side of the peninsula and another onto the north, both submerging not only buildings but also coconut palms. The two walls collided with a deafening thunderclap that dwarfed the grinding roar. White spray erupted hundreds of feet high. A bicycle twirled high in the spray, blasted into the air by the force of the impact.

This demented flood shot up the peninsula, riding over the earlier and shallower surge. It gobbled an old grandmother and a young policeman wading as fast as they could through the shallow water. Ruslan put his head down and forced his legs to sprint even faster. He turned up the road to the Old Mosque, to the boulevard that would lead away from the sea. Black water poured out of alleyways in front of him, cutting off that direction. Without breaking stride, he careened into a lane that would take him the other way, toward the gas station. A thick tongue of water surged around a corner, turning down toward him.

He spun into another lane, and then another, his path always blocked by the sudden appearance of water determined to devour him. This part of town was as familiar to him as his paint palette, but in his terror he became disoriented. He burst from a lane onto the middle of a street of two-story shop houses. The flood raced toward him from either end of the street. He ran into the first shop house on his right, pushing through the shopkeeper's family, who'd rushed downstairs to see what was going on. "Run up! Run up!" he shouted to them, and sprinted up the stairs to the family quarters on the second floor. The response he got was an angry shout from one of the teenage sons, which turned into a panicked screech as water roared into the shop.

Within seconds the flood poured onto the second floor. The water was thick with sand and muck, and gushed with extraordinary violence, smashing furniture into the walls. Ruslan struggled to the narrow flight of stairs that led up to the attic. The water followed him up the stairs and poured in through the attic's small, barred windows. Ruslan dog-paddled to stay afloat. The water lifted him higher and higher, toward the underside of the roof, which had a thick lining of insulation under the outer tiles.

God help him, he was going to be trapped and drowned like a rat. He stood on a support beam and frantically tore at the insulation. Thick chunks came away in his hands, but the water was now up to his chin. He took a deep breath just before his head became submerged, and he banged away at the roof tiles with the flat of his hand. His lungs began to burn. Several tiles at last gave way. He gripped the edges of the hole and hoisted himself up out of the water and into blessed air, which he inhaled with ragged whoops.

From the roof he could see a flood raging along several of the town's streets. Upright cars and overturned boats and uprooted trees and debris from shattered houses tumbled in the current. People were also carried along, trying to stay atop the mess, their desperate silent efforts far more chilling than their previous screaming. Ibu Ramly, the fritter seller, pushed her young son onto a floating refrigerator whose door was open. He fell inside. As she tried to climb on, the door shut on her son, and she fell into the water and did not reappear.

The roof underneath Ruslan began to quiver. The eave below him crumbled. The shop house was collapsing into the flood. Ruslan raced on his hands and knees along the cracking roofline to the adjoining shop house. He was just feet away when the beams underneath him gave way. God help him, the flood was going to get him after all. But now his fright became an instant fury. He was not going to let the water win. With one last lunge he jumped up and grabbed the base of the satellite TV dish on the edge of the neighboring rooftop. The metal pole bent under his weight. A bolt popped. Water tugged at his dangling legs and ripped away his sandals. He strained to fight off the current, scrabbling his feet against the wall. His toes found a crack, and he pushed off the tiny surface. That, and his grip on the bending pole, was enough for him to scoot over the edge of the roof.

A woman floated by, just a few feet below him. He recognized her as one of the fishmongers, clutching on to her market table. Her mouth gaped at Ruslan, her eyes blank with fright. He lay down on the sloped roof and grabbed her arm. For some reason, she tried to fight him off. He shouted at the panicked woman and heaved her up out of the water, landing her like a fish onto the rooftop beside him.

A moment later a Toyota sedan spun into view on the water. It carried on its top Haji Kamarudin, his white skullcap still plastered on his head. He noticed Ruslan and held out a beseeching hand, but he was too far away to reach. The sedan bumped into a submerged obstacle and halted, forming an eddying whirlpool. A log from a local lumber mill rolled onto the Haji's back, trapping him on top of the sedan as he and the car slowly sank, the Haji's terror-wide eyes still fixed on Ruslan, his hand still outstretched. In a moment all Ruslan could see above the water was the Haji's raised hand, waving for help, and then that too went under.

Chapter 6

Sarah barely sensed the red ants' fiery stings. She clung to the branch, staring at the ground below her.

Heights had always scared her. Whenever she stood on the edge of something taller than she was, nausea would flutter in her stomach.

Now she was fifty feet above the ground, on a tree with no branches in reach below her and a trunk too big to slide down.

"Help!" she screamed. "Help!"

Her cries were smothered by the jungle's absolute silence.

She lowered her forehead to her arm, squeezing her eyes shut. *When I open them, I'll wake up and be in my bunk.*

An ant bit her on the eyelid. That one she felt. "Ow!" She slapped it dead and all others in reach. Out of the corner of her eye, she saw a stout vine dangling behind her all the way to the ground.

Holding on to the trunk for balance, she gingerly rose to her feet. The vine drooped just out of reach. She would have to jump. She glanced at the ground far below and moaned. Something moved on the trunk near her hand. A lizard as big as her forearm, staring at her with cold eyes. She jerked her hand away. This threw her off balance. Her arms flailed. She was going to fall. In desperation, she sprang for the vine, which smacked her in the face where her mom had slapped her, the skin still tender from the blow. Her arms and legs automatically wrapped around the vine's rough bark. When her stunned senses cleared and she realized she wasn't falling, she inched her way down.

A minute later she stood with trembling legs on a tilted bed of newly exposed rock. The air reeked of stirred-up muck. Water lay in a hollow of a large boulder torn out of the hill, deep enough for her to rinse her filthy face.

Salty as seawater.

God, you idiot, it is *seawater. That was a tsunami. When you were studying about them in earth sciences with dandruffy old Mr. Andaars,*

you never thought you'd be in one, did you? You
were too busy passing notes—

Tsunami.

Peter. Dad. Mom.

"Peter!" she shouted. "Dad! Mom!"

Before, the jungle floor had been shrouded in shadow. Now sunlight poured through huge gaps in the canopy. Fallen trees sprawled at random. Boulders big as cars had mowed through their branches and scythed down smaller bushes, leaving ragged trails.

How could her parents and brother have survived?

Yet at the same time, her heart insisted they were alive.

She scrambled over tree trunks toppled across her path, sometimes walking down their lengths with arms outstretched for balance. She continued calling. "Peter! Peter! Mom! Dad!" There was no reply, not even a bird's call or an insect's chirrup. At the torn roots of one tree, a boar with enormous yellow tusks lay dead on its side. She made her way around it and climbed the fallen trunk. Through a breach torn in the jungle's shoreline, she could see the bay. Swirling blacks and browns stained the bay, the water littered with a jungle's flotsam, including entire uprooted trees. She did not spot the sailboat. The sun was a white kernel in an achingly clean sky. Had so much time already passed?

She squeezed around a tangle of vines and jumped onto the beach. Most of the sand had been stripped away, exposing sharp limestone ridges.

One high dune remained. There, resting against a rotting fishing net, sat her mother, her back toward Sarah, her tangled hair fluttering on the breeze.

Sarah dashed over. "Mom! Mom!"

Her mother regarded Sarah with a flat look of anger, as though ready to scold her for not keeping Peter safe.

Sarah stepped closer. "Mom?"

Her mother's eyes didn't track her. Her nightie was torn across the waist. Both her feet were caught in the fishing net. Her mouth was agape, and from her left nostril peeked a bubble of froth. Dried blood trailed down her forehead, having dripped from a crusted wound in the scalp. A cloud of flies buzzed around her head. Dozens had landed, probing not only the scalp wound but also her lips and eyes.

Sarah's head spun. She turned away and retched violently. When the spasms stopped, she rinsed her mouth in a limestone tidal pool and faced her mother again. More flies had gathered.

She took off her T-shirt and swatted the flies

away. Where had they come from? "Bastards!" she shouted. "Leave her alone!"

The flies circled and darted back in, patient and persistent. She swung away at them, keening in her rage. Her fury was soon spent, and she knelt in exhaustion in the sand. She studied her mother's face. The cold look was the same one that had been there when she had slapped Sarah, telling her to take Peter and run. Sarah could still feel the blow on her cheek. She waited for grief to come. It didn't. It felt as though something inside her had short-circuited.

She had to bury her mom. Protect her as best she could. She disentangled her mother's feet from the net. Her limbs were stiffening up and hard to move. "I'm sorry, Mom," she muttered, for there was no elegant way to do this. With a shove she toppled her mother's body onto the sand and then rolled it down to the shallow limestone crack at the foot of the dune. She scooped sand over her mother with her bare hands. The effort left her panting.

Not much of a burial. But only temporary, after all. Later there'd be a proper church funeral. She'd clutch a handkerchief and cry as a daughter should. Right now, she wiped sandy sweat from her forehead. Where was all this sweat coming from when her mouth was so dry?

She froze. Something was in the bushes. Just the littlest swish of leaves. Something was stealthily creeping behind the line of flattened and matted plants.

Tiger.

Sarah thought that all her fright had been used up. Not true. New fright sizzled in her veins. Her throat clogged. She stumbled backward, away from the jungle.

Surf Cat jumped from the foliage onto the sand dune. He bared his tiny fangs in a falsetto roar. Sarah burst into laughter that bordered on hysteria. She forced herself to stop.

Surf Cat meowed, pacing the sand dune, heading for the jungle and then circling around. His twitching tail seemed to be a signal to follow.

"Oh, all right," Sarah said.

The orange cat led her twenty feet into the strip of ruined jungle. She heard coughing. A blob of brown hair moved in the shadows of a tree's overturned roots. "Peter!" she cried, and broke into a run.

Peter sat in a pool of mud, his shorts filthy beyond washing. A deadfall log as big around as a garbage can lay across his lower right leg. "I can't get it off," he said with a plaintive wheeze. "I'm stuck."

Sarah hugged him. Tears came to her eyes. "Oh, God, Peter . . ."

"Could you please get it off me?"

Sarah bent to the log, digging her hands into the mud to get underneath the smaller end, which still seemed impossibly heavy. As she grunted and jerked upward, strength surged through her. She lifted the end high enough for Peter to pull back his leg, and then let the log drop with a splat.

The soft ground had prevented Peter's bone from breaking. He limped over to Surf Cat and picked him up. Rubbing the kitten's head, he asked, "Where's Mom and Dad?"

"Mom's dead. She was caught in a fishing net."

"Dead?"

"It was a tsunami, you know. Tidal wave."

"I don't believe you."

"I just *buried* her, Peter."

"Where?"

"On the beach where I found her."

"Show me."

"I'm not teasing you, okay? This is not something I would ever tease you about."

"Show me."

She showed Peter the net on the dune and the burial mound of scooped sand.

"I want to see her," Peter said.

Wordlessly, Sarah brushed sand away.

Peter studied their mother's exposed face for a moment and poked a cheek. His lower lip began to tremble, and his eyes blinked rapidly. He caught his lip between his teeth and bit hard, blanching the skin. Then he put Surf Cat down so he could kneel and kiss their mother on the cheek.

Sarah watched. *Why didn't I kiss her good-bye?* The oversight confused her. Too late now. Peter was pushing sand back into place.

"Is Dad dead too?" he asked.

"Of course not. We'd better go look for him."

Their father was a tough and capable man. He'd sailed around the world when he was younger. He'd once been marooned for a week on a South Pacific island. Another time he had sailed through a hurricane with a cracked skull. A big news write-up. Even with the printed X-ray of his cracked skull, some people refused to believe it.

A broken leg was nothing.

Sarah and Peter made their way along the beach, scrambling around boulders and over downed trees. Surf Cat trotted alongside them, pausing to sniff at dead fish. They called for their father and listened for his reply. Nothing. Only the mocking sound of small waves lapping on the ruined beach.

"Dad! Dad! Dad!" Peter shouted, his voice rising until he was shrieking.

His infectious panic incited Sarah's own. To

calm herself as well as Peter, she gathered him up and shushed him.

He pushed her away, coughing hard, his freckled face mottling with the effort. He spat out a mouthful of gunk flecked with dark spots. "I'm thirsty," he said in a wheezy voice. "Can we find something to drink?"

The sun hovered closer to the horizon and shone with relentless cheerfulness. Sarah climbed onto a boulder to look again for the sailboat. Probably smashed to bits, but still, there'd be canned food and bottled water. She swept her gaze across the bay and along the shoreline. No boat. No wreckage.

An oblong patch of orangey red rested in a clump of fallen bamboo. An unnatural-looking color—the only red that shade had been the ice chest kept on the stern of the boat. Sarah ran over and yanked the chest out.

Within was a single can of Sprite.

She popped the can and gulped the wonderful liquid.

"Hey," Peter said, grabbing her arm. "Don't drink it all."

"I'm not," she said, giving him her big sister glower.

"You hate Sprite."

She did, too. Or had. Reluctantly she handed

Peter the can. He guzzled the rest. God, he sounded so piggish.

Sarah sat down at the edge of a large wading pool to wash her mud-caked sandals.

"Hey, Sarah," Peter said, pointing over her shoulder to the bay's last finger of water.

Sarah looked. A sailboat hung in an enormous, shaggy tree. She glanced away and then back again. The *Dreamcatcher* was still there, cradled in a nest of branches, the bottom of its big keel ten feet off the ground. The boat looked undamaged, ready to sail into the air. The shorts and T-shirts from yesterday's wash were still strung on the back line.

For a giddy moment Sarah expected her father to appear on deck, wiping his greasy hands on a rag.

Chapter 7

For as far as Ruslan could see, Meulaboh had become a lake, clogged with floating debris. Roof-tops dotted the foul water, many with people stranded on top of them. In the distance survivors packed the flat roof of an unfinished three-story shopping mall.

Cries of horror and desperate prayers filled the air.

Beside Ruslan, the fishmonger gabbled a mix of Qur'anic verses and nonsense words.

The lake began to drain, the water returning to the sea at a slow, triumphant pace. The fishmonger's wooden table drifted past him, this time upside down, two of the legs broken off at the base.

Another woman lay crumpled upon the overturned table, her hands clutching one of the remaining legs, her sarong partially torn from her body.

Ruslan had no idea how long it took for the water to subside. Time had become meaningless for him. There came a point, though, when the killing sea had departed, revealing a stilled and savaged town. Across the way, Ruslan could see dozens of bodies crumpled on the second-floor stairs of the shopping mall. Several of the survivors on the roof began nudging the dead off the stairs, their bodies spinning over the sides.

The street below Ruslan was filled with rubble and crushed cars and smashed furniture and a thousand other things big and small that had been torn from their proper places, all glued into place by greasy black mud.

Directly beneath him were at least a dozen bodies half-buried in the mud.

He thought of the way the oil tanker had charged out to sea. The captain must have known what was going to happen. Ruslan felt an enormous rush of gratitude to this unknown man for having saved his father's life.

Perhaps his father was already looking for him. He had to get down and make his way to the waterfront. He lifted tiles off the roof to make a hole, stacking them to the side so that the owner could replace them. Fortunately, this house had no insulation. He could climb straight down into the attic.

"I'll help you down," he told the fishmonger.

She stared at the bodies below them and moaned again. She refused his hand.

There was nothing more Ruslan could do for her. At least she was alive.

Reaching the first floor of the shop house, Ruslan waded through knee-high sludge stinking of sewage. His feet stumbled against something soft. One of the shopkeeper's family. Beyond the doorway four of the bodies lay twisted with their faces exposed, their mouths filled with the black muck. One he recognized as a trishaw driver who sometimes took him to school. Long black hair covered a girl's face. There was something familiar to the cheeks. He brushed away the hair and rocked back on his heels as Tjut Sari, the beauty of the photocopy shop, stared up at him, her black eyes no longer flashing. He looked away for a moment, the horror of it almost too much to bear. He began to pull her out of the mud, to at least give her that dignity, but stopped tugging when he saw that she was nude, the water having stripped her of her clothes.

Finding his father. That's what he had to concentrate on. There'd be time enough for the dead later on. First, though, he needed something for his feet to protect them from all the broken glass and ripped metal. One of the nearby corpses had a pair of sandals that looked like they would fit, but he shuddered at the thought of taking them. Instead, he waded into a nearby shoe shop and plucked a pair of running shoes out of the mud. They were already ruined, so he didn't think the shop owner would mind. In fact, the shop owner was probably dead. Ruslan hoped not. When all this was over, he'd make a point of finding out, so he could explain why he took the shoes.

A Batak building contractor whom Ruslan vaguely knew lay crumpled in the basin of a water fountain. The man held a small Christian cross in his outstretched hand.

Half an hour later Ruslan had picked his way past hundreds of bodies clumped together or scattered individually. So many of these dead he knew. Some with torn limbs and sheared heads, their bodies mutilated by the smashing and swirling of cement blocks and wooden planks and tin sheets and heavy vehicles.

Half an hour—that was all it took for his emotions and senses to numb, for a corpse to become just another obstacle to make his way around. Other survivors appeared, searching for family.

Here and there wails of grief rent the air. Ruslan saw one distraught father holding a limp toddler close, and then holding her out again to examine her face before pressing her to his chest, as though his own beating heart could give life back to hers.

How was it possible that the sea could tilt on itself to destroy the land and its life?

The peninsula of Ujung Karang looked as though houses and people and vegetation and lamp-posts and wires and cars had been dumped into a giant mixer, ground up, and poured back out. The ugly, mottled water of the harbor lapped against the twisted pier.

And on the curve of shore lay the hull of the big oil tanker, sunken on its side, its enormous brass propeller glinting in the sun. Five sailors floated in the water by the propeller. Even wearing life jackets, they had died.

One of the bodies had on a mechanic's overalls.

Ruslan's blood thinned to vapor, and all the colors around him faded to the gray of those overalls.

Chapter 8

The giant tree that held the *Dreamcatcher* grew beside one of the hill's rocky outcrops.

Sarah circled the base of the tree, trying to find a way to climb it. She saw that the earthquake had toppled a much smaller tree from high on the outcrop. The top of the smaller tree had caught in the bigger one.

She hiked up the outcrop, Peter behind her. She studied the fallen tree's horizontal trunk, which looked stout and sturdy enough, a bridge to the *Dreamcatcher*. She took a step onto it and then froze. All the open air around her. The long drop. No way could she cross it. She retreated and put a hand on Peter's shoulder.

"You do it. Try to radio for help. And get some food and water."

He frowned.

"Come on, Peter, please. You know I'm scared of heights. And Dad might be on board."

The frown vanished. "Here, take Surf Cat."

He inched across the trunk, yelling out "Dad? Dad?" There was no answer, only the flapping of the clothes in the breeze. He swung aboard over the stern railing.

Sarah cupped a hand to her mouth. "Get those clothes!"

He yanked them off the line and threw them over the side. He also tossed a flat piece of paper and disappeared into the cabin.

Slow seconds passed. She was just about to call out to Peter when she heard his muffled shout, "Dad isn't here, and the radio's all wrecked—"

With a grinding of fiberglass, the boat tilted forward. Water poured out of the front cabin's hatch.

"Peter!" she screamed.

The swiveling keel snagged a branch no bigger than her arm, stopping the boat's forward slide. The *Dreamcatcher* tottered at a forty-five-degree angle. Peter bolted up onto the deck and over the stern railing.

"Phew," he said when he reached her side. "That

was close." He coughed and gave her an aggrieved look. "And Dad wasn't there."

The pockets of his filthy shorts bulged. "What do you have there?" she asked.

He pulled out a can of cat food.

"God, Peter! Of all the things. *Cat* food?"

"Surf Cat's gonna need food too," he snapped back. From his other pocket he pulled out two cans of tuna. "There. Happy?"

She rubbed his dirty hair. "Sorry. Let's go get those clothes."

The paper that Peter had tossed was the last nautical chart their father had used, which had been clipped next to the helm. A pencil line traced the route the *Dreamcatcher* had taken to the bay's anchorage. The pencil line tracked past a small black square on the map that marked a village on the other side of the island. Sarah vaguely recalled the village as a bunch of tin-roofed houses on stilts.

"I thought we'd need that," Peter said.

"Smart boy. Good thinking."

Peter held up a sealed bottle of drinking water, which had washed out of the front hatch. "Hey, look."

"Give that to me," Sarah said, but Peter darted away. He opened the seal and cap with his teeth and gulped with his lips wrapped around the top.

"Peter Bedford, you'd better save me some."

He lowered the bottle and eyed the remaining half. After pouring out a handful into his palm for Surf Cat, he handed the bottle to her.

The tepid water was the most delicious thing she'd ever drunk in her life. She sipped the last drop with reverence.

Some of the clothes he'd tossed had fallen into mud, but the rest had fallen onto rock. Sarah put on a pair of khaki shorts over her bikini bottom and changed her dirty T-shirt for a plain blue T-shirt, still smelling sweetly of detergent. Peter shucked off his shorts and put on blue jeans.

A plastic object beside a bush caught Sarah's eye. One of the stove's gas lighters, with a long blue handle. She clicked the trigger. To her delight, blue flame hissed out. They'd be able to make a fire. She glanced at the sun, lower yet to the horizon.

Peter followed her gaze. "We better find Dad before night."

They didn't. With sunset on red broil, they stumbled across a ravine cut by a small stream. The same ravine where she'd seen the elephants. The standing water in the streambed was brackish from the tsunami. Sarah followed it a little ways uphill and came to a mossy face of rock that would have been a gushing waterfall after rain, but was presently a trickle disappearing into pebbles. She tasted the water. Fresh.

To one side of the streambed, a big slab of rock tilted at an angle against a rock wall, forming an angular cave. A broad trail wound from the cave into the jungle. A well-used path, now partially covered with tsunami debris.

Sarah peered into the cave. About ten feet deep, five feet wide. Flat, sandy floor. Looked safe enough. Cozy, even. "We'll spend the night here and keep looking in the morning."

She had brought the plastic bottle with her. Using a broad rolled leaf to funnel the trickle of water, she filled up the bottle. She and Peter drank, too thirsty to worry about germs.

She refilled the bottle several times to pour the water over her head, scrubbing her hair. Slow, but wonderful. She rinsed out Peter's hair for him as well, sand and dirt and dead ants flaking off his scalp.

Everything around was too wet from the tsunami to make a fire, and she didn't want to climb higher to find dry wood. Surprisingly, she was hungry. After the day's horrible events, she thought she would have no appetite at all. Her stomach was growling, though. There were the two cans of tuna. God, plain tuna never sounded so delicious. One little problem, though. She burst out laughing.

"What's so funny?" Peter said. He sat cross-legged on the cave floor, leaning against the rock. Surf Cat was curled up in his lap.

She held up a can. "Canned tuna fish is one of the modern world's staple foods," she intoned, mimicking one of her most boring teachers. "Of course, a necessary ingredient of this staple food is the can opener."

Peter shook his head. "I'm not hungry anyway. And Surf Cat just ate a dead fish." Without warning, his face crumpled, and he began to cry. "Mom," he sobbed. "Mom. I want Mom."

The image of her mother dead in the fishing net came to Sarah's mind. She waited for the pain of her grief to come smashing through. Nothing. Maybe she was still too much in a state of shock to feel any grief.

But she was no longer hungry, that was for sure.

She put an arm around her brother. He wept into her T-shirt, coughing and sobbing. She let him cry for a minute and then said, "Think of Dad. Think how strong he is. It's okay to cry for Mom, but remember, we have to get through this. Let's be as strong as Dad."

Peter's crying eased to a few sniffles and wheezes.

Twilight thickened into night. "Better try to get some sleep, little guy."

Peter lay down on his side, his head on a pile of moss that Sarah had gathered for him. He cradled Surf Cat to his chest and shut his eyes.

Sarah used her sandals for a pillow. She was sore from feet to neck. What didn't ache, itched. The rising moon coated the ragged jungle and lonely streamed with silver light. Insects chirped and buzzed—all those scuttling feet and clacking jaws. It occurred to her this was the first night in her life without electricity of any kind. Not even a flashlight.

A bug crawled up her leg. She slapped it away with a shiver.

She thought of her father. Where was he? How was he spending the night?

She stood and slipped into her sandals, peering out to the nightscape. The fallen trees and torn branches floating in the bay looked like mutant creatures.

Peter coughed again.

He's going to need a doctor.

Her father's voice was taut with urgency. He spoke so distinctly that she jerked her head around. "Dad?"

That path should take you to the village.

"But what about you?"

Take care of Peter first. He's getting sick and needs a doctor. Go!

She shook Peter's shoulder. His skin felt hot, hotter than it would be from just the sun. Sarah expected him to protest about leaving their father, but he said nothing. In the bright moonlight they made their way around several fallen logs. They climbed over the last one. Before them stretched a clear path, the jungle pressing close on either side.

Sarah paused, her heart beating hard.

Tsunami or not, jungle creatures were still searching for prey to eat.

Sarah wanted to retreat to the relative safety of the cave, but she clicked the gas lighter. Waving the blue flame in warning, she started down the path, holding her brother's hand.

Chapter 9

Ruslan sprinted down to the seawall. In those few strides, he noticed that the body in the gray overalls had a thick neck and a bald head. It wasn't his father.

Still, that didn't mean his father hadn't been trapped within the ship.

Another sailor stood on the seawall.

"My father?" Ruslan asked him. "Where's my father? Yusuf the mechanic. He was working on the tanker."

"They're all dead. All of them, dead." The sailor strode away, chanting "Dead. Dead. Dead."

Ruslan squatted and wrapped his arms around his head as though that would stop his heart from ripping in half.

His elbow rubbed against a lump in his shirt pocket. Something about that lump penetrated to his stricken mind. It was the note from his father. He opened it as carefully as he could with his trembling fingers.

The scribbled writing was still legible.

> I'm not going to work on the tanker. I'm going to Ie Mameh. Your mother's relatives have asked me to come. I didn't want to tell you last night and worry you. You look like you haven't been getting enough sleep as it is. Don't worry about me. I should be home by evening. I'll let you know.
> Don't worry, I'll be fine.

Any other day except this one, Ruslan would have indeed worried, despite his father's underlining. The hill village of Ie Mameh was considered rebel territory, where rebels were fighting for an independent Aceh state. In fact, Ruslan had heard rumors that his mother's relatives were themselves rebels. Over the years, military intelligence officers had periodically summoned Ruslan's father for questioning. So, sure, any other day except this one, he would have been terribly worried.

But on *this* day, with dead sailors floating around the oil tanker, the note filled him with such overwhelming relief that he cried. He blubbered like a baby. When he finally dried his tears, he had only one thing in mind: He had to get to Ie Mameh.

The shortest way was via Calang, a sleepy harbor town fifty miles north of Meulaboh, and then a road into the hills.

He made his way across the ruins of Ujung Karang to the main road heading north to Calang. Thick sand covered the road. A battered minibus lay toppled on its side. Ruslan started to climb onto the bus for a better look, but then noticed the crush of bodies within. He climbed instead a remnant of wall.

The bridge spanning the northern estuary had been ripped off its concrete base, its metal span flung to the side.

There was a back way, an old logging trail. It began somewhere around the farming village of Bergang, ten miles inland.

First things first, then. He had to get to Bergang, and the surest way to do that was to start walking.

The sea had flooded nearly all the way to the hospital. This inland part of town was untouched by water, but bubbled with chaos. People ran around in distress, dodging vehicles that seemed to be doing nothing but turning around in circles, their drivers uncertain where to go.

In an alley, Ruslan spotted a trail bike lying on its side, keys still dangling in the ignition. It would be perfect for the logging road. He'd borrow it and return it later to its owner with apologies. There wasn't a helmet for him to wear, but sometimes in an emergency one had to take chances. Nobody stopped him as he righted the bike and checked the fuel. Empty. Just down the block was an unattended kiosk that sold gasoline in glass bottles. He filled up the bike's tank and took two spare bottles, putting them in a canvas knapsack that had been resting on the counter. He'd pay the kiosk owner later.

Ten minutes later he was blasting down a smooth road winding through rice paddies. Their green serenity seemed to Ruslan to be another world.

On the outskirts of Bergang a farmer on the way to his fields gave directions to the logging road turn-off. "Be careful," he said. "Rebels are in that area."

Ruslan found the turnoff, an unpaved slash of orange dirt leading into a rubber plantation. Two privates from the military's Raider division were seated in a wooden guard hut at the foot of a small, shrub-covered hill. On the top of the hill stood a sandbagged command post. As soon as the privates saw Ruslan, they lowered a bamboo gate across the trail.

What was he going to say?

He said the first thing that came to mind. "Meulaboh's been flooded out by the sea. People are dead everywhere."

One of the privates blew cigarette smoke. "What are you talking about?"

"The town's destroyed. So many dead people." His voice quavered. The soldiers stared at him.

"You're crazy," said the second private.

"I'm not crazy. I tell you, the town's gone. Bodies everywhere, drowned, smashed up."

"Let's see your ID card."

Ruslan took out the laminated identity card from his damp wallet. The soldier studied it, compared Ruslan's face to the small photo, and said, "I think you'd better talk to our commander."

Ruslan parked the bike in a small lot behind the hill, hanging his backpack off the handlebars. He palmed the ignition key. One of the soldiers escorted him up the hill and into a room with two bunk beds, a desk, and a radio set. An officer sat at the desk with a cell phone in his hand, punching buttons in irritation. Ruslan could hear the squeal of disrupted service. The officer cursed.

The private handed the officer Ruslan's ID card.

"There's been a flood in Meulaboh," Ruslan said. "Most of Meulaboh's gone, I tell you. Smashed to pieces by a giant ocean wave. So many dead."

The officer was just as skeptical as the private. "Is that so?"

"Look at me. My shoes are wet, my jeans are wet, I nearly drowned."

The officer grunted. His leathery face held the natural suspicion that all field officers had. "You rebels should learn to tell a better story."

The officer's skepticism made Ruslan wonder if in fact he was somehow imagining it all. Yet specks of that awful black muck still dotted his forearms.

"I'm not a rebel," Ruslan said. "I'm a good citizen. You can ask anybody."

"Don't worry, we will." The officer put Ruslan's ID card in his pocket. He got up and left the room, his last words a command to the private to keep an eye on Ruslan. The private ordered Ruslan to squat in the corner.

Ruslan thought quickly. Once they found out he was the son of Yusuf the mechanic, who had possible rebel connections, military intelligence would interrogate him. They had ways to make one speak. And if they then found out from him that Yusuf the mechanic was in rebel country, then who knew what trouble would come to Ruslan and his father?

It was crazy to be thinking about such things when Meulaboh had been flattened and thousands had drowned.

Still, there it was.

Ruslan made a wincing face. "I have to go to the bathroom. Diarrhea."

"Out there," the private said, gesturing through the open door to the latrine within the sandbagged perimeter.

As Ruslan had hoped, the tin sheet wall of the latrine wasn't securely fixed to the wooden frame. He worked one side open and squeezed through. After putting the ignition key in his mouth for quick access, he climbed over the sandbag embankment and skidded on his rear down the hill's steep slope to the trail bike.

Above him, he heard the private's cry of alarm.

Ruslan felt surprisingly calm as he put on his backpack and swung onto the bike. He inserted the ignition key and thumbed the engine switch. The bike roared to life. He goosed it around in a tight circle, but he'd forgotten about the kickstand, which caught in the dirt. The bike wobbled, nearly throwing him. He wrestled the handlebars, losing precious seconds, but managed to get the bike under control. He flicked up the kickstand with his right heel as he opened the throttle, speeding out onto the trail. Behind him, he heard shouts and the loud cracks of rifles. The ground to the side and front of him exploded in a shower of dirt. They weren't shooting to warn him. Bending low to the handlebars, he raced into the rubber grove.

Within a minute he was lost in the unending ranks of trees. He braked to a stop to orient himself.

Shouts in the distance. He sped off in the opposite direction.

The ditch came up unseen, camouflaged by thick weeds. He flew off the handlebars and lay stunned on hard ground. Gasoline trickled down his neck, the scent of it making him woozier. A bottle in his pack had broken, but as he took dazed inventory of his body parts, he himself seemed intact.

He sat up and found himself looking down the length of a ragged, unpaved road, the hardpan dirt crevassed by the rain runoff. Here the rubber plantation gave way to the dense scrub trees that marked a logged forest, the scraggly trees bending over the road, almost making a tunnel.

He'd found the old logging trail.

The bike's electric thumb start was smashed. He cranked the kick start. No luck. The faint growling of a Jeep filtered through the trees.

Another crank. Nothing. He bent over to the side and looked. The cap to the spark plug was loose. He crammed it on tight. This time the bike started just as the hood of a Jeep smashed through some weeds. Jamming the bike into gear, he roared off, zigzagging around crevasses. He came to a wash-out too steep for any four-wheel vehicle to traverse. Almost too much for the bike as well, but he managed to tug and wrench it down and then back up the eroded contours. Another washout followed, and then a third.

An hour later his arms felt as though they were going to come off. His thigh muscles ached. His stomach hurt. Who would have thought riding a bike could be such hard work? He'd never done anything so physical in his life and so demanding of relentless concentration. His brain was about as wrung out as his muscles. Only to cover five miles.

But he was five miles closer to Ie Mameh.

When dusk came, he'd been hours riding through boggy lowland. He drove the bike onto a spit of higher ground and got off. His arms and hands continued to vibrate. Squatting by a pool of stagnant water, he washed dirt off his face. That done, he lay down close to the bike, using his knapsack as a pillow. He'd forgotten about the broken bottle, though, and fished out the pieces. He also found two tangerines. After washing and peeling them, he squatted by the trail bike and sucked the sections one by one. He chewed the pulp, spitting out the seeds, idly aiming for a lump of submerged moss the size of his head in the water.

As he spat out the last seed, he noticed that the lump was making the slightest of ripples in the water. In fact, the lump was attached to what he'd taken for a twisted, mossy log, which was itself rippling ever so gently.

He noticed then the python's eyes, focused intently on him.

Chapter 10

In the moonlight, Sarah could see only a few steep yards of the jungle path before her. She had no idea how long she and Peter had been hiking. They had already crested several hills, and each time she thought that they'd be descending to the village on the other side of the island. But there was always another hill waiting.

This particular climb seemed endless. Each step required complete concentration. She had to calculate where to place her feet to avoid ankle-twisting ruts or slippery clay. Which branch or rock to hang on to for balance. There was Peter to help, as well.

A big tree root had grown across the path. She took Peter's hand and helped him over it. No sooner had he stepped down on the other side than the bush beside them rustled with a shaking of leaves. She halted, holding her panting breath, and fired the stove lighter. The blue flame reflected off two eyes glowing in the foliage. She screamed.

Several piglets bolted from the bush and scurried across the path. An adult boar emerged and stopped in the path, facing Sarah with a menacing stance, its sharp tusks gleaming in the moonlight. Sarah jabbed the flame at the boar. She could feel her heart hammering, but the only sound in the night was the flame's little hiss. The boar didn't budge, its eyes jerking from Sarah to Peter and back to Sarah again.

When the last of the piglets was safely hidden on the other side of the path, the boar sprinted into the jungle.

"Phew," Sarah said. She sat down on the tree root. She was drenched with sweat. Peter slumped beside her. Surf Cat bounded over the root and meowed impatiently, as if chiding them for stopping.

"Darn cat's worse than Dad," Sarah muttered.

Peter put his forehead on his crossed arms.

Sarah had been rationing the bottle of water. There was a quarter left. She swallowed half and handed the bottle to Peter.

When he'd finished, she took the empty bottle from him. "Come on, let's go."

"I'm so tired. Can't we have a little break?"

"You know what Dad would say," she said with fake sternness.

"Yeah. The journey of a thousand miles begins with a nap."

Sarah chuckled. "True. But he was talking about Mom. Whenever there's something to do, Dad does it until it's done. So come on."

Peter took a deep, wheezy breath and stood.

Just that little bit of water helped. They made it to the top of the ridge, and Sarah could at last see the ocean's pale glitter. The moon was halfway to the western horizon. They'd been hiking almost all night. The path led along the ridge for a few hundred yards and then turned downhill to the village.

An hour later, halfway down to the seashore, the fiery red sun rose full above the eastern horizon even before the pale round moon had touched the western one. Sarah had never seen the sun and moon in the sky at the same time. The sight was unnerving, almost alien.

One more knoll stood below them, blocking the view of the shore and the village. Tops of coconut palms poked above the knoll. This sight soothed Sarah's uneasiness. They'd soon have food and water. A village doctor who could treat Peter. A search party for their dad.

On a plateau before the knoll, the path narrowed through a field of tall grass. A shack stood on the edge of the field. One portion of the grass had been harvested, probably for roofing thatch.

By the time they reached the field, the moon had sunk into the sea and the sun had risen above it. She pushed her way through the grass. When she exited, she noted several small black leaves plastered to the backs of her knees. She reached down to idly brush one off. It remained stuck to her skin. She pinched it to remove it, but what her fingers squeezed was something soft. Rubbery. She took a closer look. Not a leaf. A leech, plumping up by the second with her blood. As were the other ones.

Her skin crawled. She yelped, slapping at the leeches with her fingers but not wanting to touch them either.

Peter bent over to examine his legs. "Hey, I got 'em too. They don't hurt you. Mr. Tuttle says so." Mr. Tuttle was his science teacher. "They'll drink up and fall off. They use 'em in medicine, you know."

"They're gross!" Sarah cried. She clicked the gas lighter and carefully brought the tip of the blue flame to each leech. "Die, you suckers." They writhed and fell off. She turned the gas lighter to Peter.

"No, no, let 'em be," he said.

"God, Peter, I don't want to be around somebody who's got leeches all over him. Hold still. I don't want to burn you."

The leeches' bites continued to bleed as they started walking up the knoll's gentle incline. "They got this chemical that stops your blood from cagulating," Peter said.

"Coagulating," Sarah said automatically, and shuddered again. "Disgusting." As they approached the top of the knoll, she started imagining the villagers' response to two white kids with blood on their legs appearing out of nowhere. Would anyone know English? But it'd be easy enough to mime for a drink of water. And "doctor" was a universal word. So was "papa."

The first thing that came into view was the sea, the distant blue giving way to mottled brown water ringing the island. And then the shoreline, curving several hundred yards between two ridges of tumbling rock. The narrow shore was empty, scoured up to the edge of the jungle and several coconut groves. Brown mud glistened, lapped by murky waves.

The village was gone.

Chapter 11

The python gathered speed. Ruslan realized that in his squatting position he looked like something tasty and easy to swallow. He scrambled to his feet, backing up to the trail bike, but too late. The python sprang, its jaws missing Ruslan's leg but biting the cuff of his jeans. The rest of the giant snake whipped up to coil around him. Ruslan spun and pressed the snake's blunt head against the bike's hot exhaust pipe. At once the python let go and writhed away into the water.

Ruslan got back on the trail bike and rode for another hour into the night, his world condensed down to the beam of his headlight. The bog finally dried up and the trail climbed to scrubby dry ground. He braked to a halt on a level patch of rock and scree and turned the bike handle left and right, using the headlight as a search beam. All he could see was ordinary brush.

After he swung off the bike, the delayed reaction to the python attack finally set in. Drowning was one thing, but being eaten was another. He trembled violently for at least a minute before he could say his evening prayers. When they were finished, he spread out on the ground as close as he could to the bike, tucking his head into the gap between the front wheel and engine, using the knapsack as a pillow. He fell sound asleep, too bone tired for any dreams or nightmares. When he woke, stiff as the flat rock he had slept on, it was already dawn. He peed into a bush and with a groan swung his sore body onto the trail bike. How much farther did he have to go? If he remembered correctly, the logging track would at some point turn back down to the coast and end at Teunom, a village beside a river mouth. There he could get something to eat and drink before continuing on to Calang and Ie Mameh. He didn't have any money, but by now the people at Teunom surely knew of the disaster that had befallen Meulaboh and would help him.

The trail was a jarring path of ridges and ruts. Eventually the path widened into a potholed road that wound along the side of the lowest foothill. He came to an intersection. The right-hand fork led back up into the hills. To where, Ruslan didn't know. He chose the fork that descended through oil palms to the flat coastal plains and the main road to Calang.

At the bottom of the hill a spring burbled out of the rocks, forming a small pool. Ruslan stopped. He waded out into the pool and cupped his hands at the spring to drink. His thirst at last slaked, he turned and sank into the waist-high water for a good soak.

He froze. In the wattle brush lining the far end of the pool, a man stared at him with wide and bulging eyes.

Unblinking eyes, rigid with death.

Around him were several more corpses, caught in the brush like debris.

The flood had struck here, too.

Ruslan drove on. Fallen trees and mounds of swamp muck made the driving difficult, and then, after half a mile, impossible. He pushed the trail bike into the crown of a downed oil palm, camouflaging it as best he could with the leaves.

A shadow of a man holding a rifle fell before him. Another shadow appeared, and then a third. Ruslan spun around.

A band of five armed men in civilian clothes had

materialized out of the destroyed land. Lurking in the backs of their eyes was something as hard and hollow as the barrels of their well-oiled rifles.

Rebels.

One of the men had a dead eye, nothing but a white swirl. He didn't speak. A man with a livid scar on his forearm nodded at the hidden bike. "What you doing with that motorbike, boy?"

"Trying to keep it safe," Ruslan said. "I borrowed it. It's not mine."

"That's right. It's ours now. Give me your bag."

Ruslan handed him the knapsack, which the man checked and returned. "Where you come from?"

"Meulaboh. It's been destroyed by the flood. I came along the old logging trail."

"We saw your headlights last night. The military let you pass their checkpoints?"

The question sounded idle, but Ruslan sensed a trap. The rebels trusted no one they did not know. The military employed all sorts of agents and informants, from grandmothers to fresh-faced schoolkids.

"My father is Yusuf the mechanic," he said. "He's gone to Ie Mameh. That's where I'm going, to find him. Meulaboh's destroyed." He gestured at the ruined land around them. "Just like here. A monster sea wave."

The man glanced at the white-eyed man. "Ie Mameh, is that right? Now, why would a mechanic from Meulaboh be going to Ie Mameh? They have their own mechanics there."

"That's where my mother's from. Her relatives asked him to come."

"Let's see your ID."

Ruslan thought of his ID card, tucked away in the officer's pocket. "I lost it."

"What's that in your back pocket?" Ruslan handed him his wallet. The man inspected its contents. "Why would you have your wallet and not your ID?"

Ruslan opened his mouth to lie that the ID card had been in his shirt pocket, but instead other words rose to his tongue before he could stop them. "You're worried about my ID? Look around you! Look what's happened!"

Another man spat. "We don't have time for this. Let's just shoot him." He aimed his rifle at Ruslan's chest, his finger tightening on the trigger.

Chapter 12

Sarah stared at the empty shoreline. Oh dear God, the tsunami had surged around the whole island and torn out the village. Not a stick remained.

Peter threw himself down onto a patch of soft grass and was instantly asleep.

Sarah licked her dry lips. What was she going to do now?

A few miles to the west, black smoke drifted into the big blue sky. Smoke from a fishing boat, heading toward the island.

Sarah laughed and clapped her hands. Then she realized that the boat's present course would take it a good ways offshore. She stopped clapping. She had to do something to catch its attention. A fire. Plenty of dry wood here for a big one. She'd throw in green branches to make billows of signaling smoke.

She rushed about, gathering moss, twigs, and leaves for the starter fire as her father had taught her years ago on a camping trip. She arranged this material in a pit she scooped out with her hands. On top of that she layered larger sticks and waited for the boat to draw closer. No point in starting the fire too soon.

The boat grew bigger. The dull beat of its engine became audible on the breeze. Sarah knelt by the prepared stack with the gas lighter. The blue flame licked the twigs, which blazed for a moment before dying out. She rearranged the material in the pit and clicked the lighter's trigger. No flame. Another click. Still no flame. She shook the lighter and pulled the trigger again and again and again.

She'd used up the last of the lighter's gas burning off those leeches.

With an angry cry she hurled the lighter into the bushes. Tears of frustration streaked her cheeks. She raced down to the shoreline and waved and shrieked as the boat chugged past a half mile offshore. It held its course and all too soon presented its disappearing stern to her.

She sank to her knees in the mud. A big blank

nothingness rose up around the edges of her mind, threatening to swallow it up. There weren't even any more tears.

"Dad," she whispered.

Her father's calm voice came to her. *Look at Surf Cat, playing with those coconuts.*

She focused her gaze on Surf Cat, who was in a nearby palm grove planted in a jungle clearing. The cat stood on his hind legs beside an uprooted palm tree, swatting a dangling green coconut with his paws. God, after everything that had happened, the cat could still play? Then it struck her: coconut. Lots of them in the fallen crown of the tree, in easy reach. Sarah made her way over and twisted one of the young nuts off its stem.

Now what? It was the tuna can all over again. She had to find something to open it with.

She paced along the shore, scanning the ground for any sharp object she could use. Nothing. She came to the rocky ridge that had marked the village's northern boundary. Now, here was stone. Lots of stone. She recalled the time Mrs. Koenigswald had brought into her history class a professional knapper, a person who made blades out of stone, as people had done thousands of years ago. God, who would have thought that such a skill could still come in handy? She should have paid closer attention.

She picked up a rock the size of a football and threw it as hard as she could against a boulder. The rock bounced away.

Wait a second. Why not smash the coconut itself? She climbed the ridge, looking for a suitable spike in the rock to puncture and tear the nut's tough hide. Beyond the ridge was an inlet, a keyhole packed with spiky-legged mangrove trees. There'd be nothing there for her.

She was just turning away when she noticed out of the corner of her eye something rocking back and forth between two of the mangrove trees. A wooden boat, its narrow open hull about ten feet long, rocking in the incoming tide. A blue plastic sail was furled around two long pieces of bamboo.

She made her way down the other side of the ridge and waded out in the mangrove muck to the boat. The few inches of water underneath the floorboards stank of fish. A paddle rested on the cross plank that served as the seat, as though the fisherman had casually left it there minutes ago.

"Hello, hello?" she called, but only the clicking of crabs answered her.

A wooden handle was stuck behind one of the rib planks. She reached across the hull but didn't have the leverage to pull it out. The hull listed as she clambered over the side. She tugged on the handle, and the rest of it appeared, a fisherman's cleaver with silver fish scales dotting its dark blade. She whooped in delight. From the Stone Age to the Iron Age, just like that! She bent over the side of the boat to wash the machete in the water before hacking open the coconut. Even with a stout blade, it was harder than it seemed, the coconut repeatedly spinning out of her hand onto the floorboards. When she had bared part of the hard brown shell, it cracked in the wrong place, and coconut milk sloshed into the dirty bilge.

"No!" she said, quickly righting the nut. Fortunately, the remaining milk, sweet as heaven, slaked the burning edge of her thirst. She whacked open the rest of the nut to scoop the soft meat out with her fingers.

The quiet was suddenly shattered by Peter's faint but hysterical screams rising from the other side of the ridge. "Sarah! Sarah! Where are you? Sarah!"

She grabbed the oar. Fear galvanized her awkward paddling. "I'm coming!" she shouted. His screams ceased, and her imagination feared the worst. A tiger.

"He's okay, he's okay, he's okay," she chanted as she stroked. When she rounded the point, she saw him on the shore, bent over and coughing hard from his screaming. She stopped paddling, limp with relief. He looked up at her, and she waved the oar. He was still pale from his fright, but trying not to show it now.

"Look what I found," she said, patting the hull.

"We're going to go in that?"

She looked at the empty horizons and up at the fair-weather clouds scudding across the blue sky. She noticed too how Peter was beginning to flush with fever. "Yup."

She chopped open two more coconuts for her and Peter. He drank the milk but said he wasn't hungry for the meat.

"Eat," she said.

"You sound just like Mom."

"No dessert until you do," she said.

He smiled and ate a few scoops. When he was done, he helped her gather the rest of the coconuts off the fallen palm and stock them in the boat. While Peter rested, she searched along the edge of the jungle and found a type of wild, fruitless banana tree with long broad leaves. She cut down half a dozen leaves and put them in the boat to provide shade. She unfurled the plastic sail. It took her a while to figure out how it worked. One pole remained upright in a hole in the boat's forward crossbeam, while the other skewed at an angle, stretching out the triangular sail. A line—*a sheet*, she heard her father say—was tied to the second pole, and this held the sail steady to the wind.

"I guess we're ready to go," she called out to Peter.

He boarded and crouched in the front of the hull, holding Surf Cat in his lap. She pushed off the beach, the sail flapping in the mild breeze. When she hauled on the sheet, the boat tilted to the side and surged forward with surprising speed.

"You sure we're going the right way?" Peter asked.

God, how stupid of her. She hadn't thought of that. She studied the lay of the island, the sun, and the direction of the boat. As far as she could calculate, they were headed in the right direction for that last town they'd been in. Out on the horizon was a haze that could only be the tops of clouds over Sumatra's mountains.

"Malibu, here we come," she said.

"Huh?" Peter said. "Malibu?"

"Where we got the engine fixed."

"Meulaboh—*meh-lah-boh*."

"Okay, *meh-lah-boh*, Mr. Smarty Pants. You can speak to the natives when we get there."

She tied the sheet off on a peg obviously meant for that purpose. Peter gazed brightly around him and then seemed to instantly run out of energy and curiosity, curling up before the sail post with bent knees, his head cradled on his hands. She put several of the banana leaves over him to protect him from the sun and stuck another inside one of the boat planks to give herself a strip of shade.

"Can you feed Surf Cat for me?" Peter asked.

Using the tip of the machete, Sarah pried open a hole in the can of cat food. She thought about opening a can of tuna, but decided to save the tuna for when they didn't have coconut. Surf Cat ate all the cat food and then fearlessly crouched on the bow of the boat to lick his fur.

The boat sailed itself, putting down a straight thin wake. With nothing to do, Sarah became conscious of her dirty teeth. She had always been particular about brushing and flossing before bed, and now her teeth felt mossy and all gunked up. It drove her crazy. She rubbed them with her forefinger and scratched them with her nails, but that didn't satisfy her. A piece of nylon fishing line wound around one of the boat's ribs. She picked it off, washed it over the side in the sea, and used it as floss. When she was done with that, she used the tip of the machete to dig out dirt from underneath her fingernails. She hadn't had a chance to do them.

Behind them, Tiger Island dwindled, and around

them, the sea changed from brown to the blue of open ocean, a color that made the hull seem awfully small. She scanned the horizon, hoping to see a ship.

And there, a smokestack, rising from a funnel—she jerked upright, blinking her bleary eyes to clear them. The dream vessel had vanished. She splashed water on her face to stay awake, but her tiredness pulled her head down onto her arms, the heat and the boat's rhythmic motion lulling her back to sleep.

A thud woke her. Two enormous claws rose out of the water, accompanied by a rapid huffing noise. For a second she thought this too was a lingering dream, but the claws didn't vanish. She screamed, sure that a sea monster was attacking them. But it wasn't a sea monster. The claws were hooves that scrabbled up onto the side of the hull, tilting it to the water. Then the water buffalo's face appeared, its reddened eyes round with fear as it tried to climb aboard the tiny boat.

Chapter 13

Ruslan stared at the end of the gun barrel aimed at his chest. It didn't have a flash suppressor, and the hole looked so big that he imagined he could see the grooves that would spin the bullet into his heart. After all he'd been through, this was how he was going to die? If he weren't so scared, he'd be laughing at the absurdity.

"Wait." A word of command, spoken by the man with the dead white eye.

The other rebel lowered his rifle.

The man strode up to Ruslan. His dead eye seemed as penetrating as his good one. "Your father is Yusuf the mechanic, you said? And he went to his wife's relatives in Ie Mameh?"

Ruslan nodded, his legs trembling at this sudden reprieve. He tried to hold them still, not wanting the rebels to see how frightened he'd been.

One of the rebels laughed and pointed at Ruslan's crotch. "Look. He's peed himself."

Ruslan looked down. A big, fresh wet spot marked the front of his drying jeans. His face burned with shame.

"Aw, little boy," the man who'd pointed the gun said. "You didn't think I'd really shoot you, did you?"

The leader said, "What's your mother's name?"

"Tjut Intan," Ruslan mumbled. "She was a schoolteacher."

"What happened to her?"

"She was killed in a firefight when I was three."

The leader murmured with the scarred man and then told Ruslan, "You come with us."

"Where?"

"Wherever we tell you."

"But I need to get to Ie Mameh."

The leader's smile didn't reach his good eye. "You're with us now. We're your family. We need a pair of strong shoulders like yours. Lots of stuff to carry."

Ruslan knew that rebels occasionally forced young males into service, sometimes for months. He had to escape from these men. He had to get to Ie Mameh. But for now, he had to play it smart and go along.

They gave him a zippered gym bag to carry that was as heavy as a rock. What was inside? Ammunition for the rifles? Grenades? He hiked in the middle of the group, the men spread out and keeping a casual but close eye on him. They came to a destroyed village, houses obliterated down to the foundations, with trails of smashed bricks and tiles pointing like arrows away from the coastline. The rebels scavenged through the debris. They found a carton of bottled water, the seals unbroken. These they divided among themselves, two each. The leader made sure Ruslan got his share, which he put in his knapsack on his back.

The scarred rebel found a gold headdress in a broken wardrobe. He unzipped Ruslan's gym bag to put the headdress inside. Other gold objects glittered within. There were also wads of money.

Ruslan said nothing.

They came to two bodies, a shirtless man, a woman in sarong and headdress. The scarred rebel patted the male's pockets. He shook his head. But the female had a gold chain that he unfastened from her neck and handed to Ruslan.

Ruslan backed away in horror. "This is sacrilege!"

The leader turned to Ruslan, piercing him with

that dead eye. "If we don't take it now, somebody else will take it later. There are survivors with us we must feed. Take the chain."

The scarred rebel held his rifle as though ready to use it on Ruslan for real this time.

Ruslan added the chain to his bag.

The leader stood over the corpses and murmured a quick prayer.

The band made their way along a littered road to the edge of a broad brown river twirling away to the coast and the small town of Teunom. Even this far inland the bridge's roadway had been torn out by the force of the flood, but one metal beam, and the cable that supported it with guy wires, still spanned the hundred yards to the other side of the river. The first rebel slung his rifle over his shoulder and climbed up onto the girder to start crossing.

An idea popped into Ruslan's mind. He faked a shudder. "I can't swim."

The scarred man patted his shoulder. "You're not swimming."

"What if I fall?"

"Good point. I'd better take that bag."

Ruslan was third onto the girder, a metal I-beam whose flat top was the width of his hands. Wide enough, with the cable's guy wires offering good handholds. But in the middle of the crossing, Ruslan no longer had to fake his nervousness. The river below seemed so far away, its brown eddies deep and powerful. He almost abandoned his idea, but he knew he'd never have another chance to escape these men and get to Ie Mameh. He took several deep breaths and pretended to slip. He wailed with a flailing of arms and let himself fall backward into the air.

The drop seemed endless. He hit the water with a painful smack. The rebels on the girder shouted down at him. He remembered he was playing a role and splashed ineffectively for a few moments before ducking under the opaque surface and letting the current carry him for as long as his breath could hold.

Several minutes later he'd been swept around a curve and out of sight of the bridge. He kept to the deepest, strongest part of the river. The swirling energy of this water was nothing compared to what he'd lived through in Meulaboh. Its current slowed as the river opened up onto a wide estuary. Ruslan began swimming awkwardly in his jeans and shoes to the high northern bank, beyond which lay Teunom.

Several bodies floated in shoreline reeds. Ruslan ignored them. The dead, it seemed, would now be as much a part of his life as the living had been.

After he squished up the opposite bank, it took only one glance to know there was no more Teunom, no more farmers tending to their fields, no more fishermen hauling their catch to market.

Twenty miles to the north rose the coastal hills of Calang. From where Ruslan stood he could see that the highway along the coast had been ripped apart, great slabs of asphalt torn up and tossed aside. It'd be easier to walk along the beach. He drank one of the bottles of water from his knapsack and trudged along the riverbank to the shoreline.

For a mile out to sea, the waters were still brown and streaked with long patches of foam. The beach's soft gray sand spilled hot into his wet shoes. Muddy waves rose and crashed in foam that hissed up toward his feet. One wave larger than the others wobbled up out of the depths, and in Ruslan's imagination its brown darkened to black as it rose and rose and rose.

He turned and ran, screaming.

Chapter 14

Sarah pounded the water buffalo's head with the oar as water poured into the tilted hull.

"Peter, help!" she screamed.

He kicked at the closest hoof. Sarah swung the oar again. It broke in half on the creature's head. She threw down the pieces and picked up the machete, using the flat of the blade to smack its nose. At the same time, Peter gave its snout a hard shove with his foot. The buffalo's front hooves slipped off the boat. Sarah paddled furiously with the broken oar to get away, the half-submerged boat heavy in the water. The buffalo swam after the boat, but it couldn't keep up, the waves swamping its massive head, which sank lower and lower in the water. Finally the head sank altogether and didn't come back up.

Sarah stopped paddling and hung her head, panting hard to catch her breath. She felt sorry for the beast, but what else could she have done?

"What was that water buffalo doing way out here?" Peter asked.

"Maybe a boat sank."

The sheet had loosened on its peg, and the sail flapped. The sun blazed overhead. She'd been asleep at the wheel—*helm*, she heard her father say—for at least three hours. Tiger Island was a blob in the distance, and the opposite horizon was filled with a glorious sight, the mountains, foothills, and plains of the Sumatran mainland.

Using coconut shells, she and Peter scooped water out of the hull before she set the sail again. The boat headed for a cluster of small hills rising from the distant shoreline. She couldn't recall if Malibu, or however it was pronounced, had such hills, but that didn't matter. Wherever she landed, there were bound to be people who would help.

Did they know yet about the disaster that had swept Tiger Island?

She and Peter shared another coconut. He drank the slightly sweet milk, sipping between bouts of coughing.

"We're almost there," she said. "We'll get you to a doctor and then I'll go back and look for Dad. Lie down. You need to rest."

Peter didn't argue. He curled up around the sail post. Sarah adjusted the leaves over him, protecting him from the sun.

The blue of the sea changed back again to shades of mottled brown. The boat bumped into an object. A man, floating facedown. She seized the closest arm. Cold and pudgy. With a shiver, she let go. Several more bodies bobbed into view, another man and two women. The man was shirtless, the women partially nude. The last one had her arm over something. The boat's bow wake rolled over her, and her arm slid off the bundle. A small girl.

Sarah put a hand to her mouth to stop from crying out. She no longer thought a boat had sunk. She was beginning to suspect the truth. The boat sailed through the awful flotsam of several more bodies and other odd debris. A round yellow water tank. Cushions. A floating fridge. An upside-down table, with a body crumpled on top of it. The body stirred and croaked for help. Sarah let the sail flutter and paddled back in a hard circle to come alongside the table. She helped the woman slither into the hull. Her sarong and blouse were ripped, her headdress skewed. Once in the hull, the woman didn't move, breathing shallowly and licking her cracked lips. Sarah began to cut open a coconut to give her something to drink.

A sharp flare of life returned to the woman's dried-out gaze. She seized the machete from Sarah's hands and in seconds had chopped open the coconut. She guzzled the nut, shaking it for the last remaining drops. "*Terima kasih*," she said to Sarah, thanking her. She seemed to have no curiosity at all about why a white girl would be sailing a small fisherman's boat hardly bigger than a canoe. The woman squatted to eat the meat, and when that was done, she picked up one of the banana leaves draped over the front of the boat to stare for a moment at Peter. She carefully replaced the leaf and gave Sarah a brief, sympathetic look. She said something that Sarah didn't understand.

"I need to find a doctor for him," Sarah told her.

The wind had shifted. The boat would land well south of the hills. The shore drew nearer. Sarah eyed the shoreline, a long stretch of gray sand, surf foaming at its edge.

The banana leaves stirred, and Peter sat up. The woman shrieked, a hand clasped to her throat as she stared with fright at Peter.

"Oh," Sarah said, with sudden understanding. "He wasn't dead, just sleeping." She put her hands together and rested her cheek on them to illustrate. "Sleeping."

The woman relaxed and studied Peter. She scooted forward on the hull's floorboards and gave him a hug. He was drowsily confused at first, but then leaned against her. She felt his forehead, her brow furrowing at his fever. She said something to Sarah, clearly a question, but Sarah could only shrug and say, "I'm sorry, I don't know what you're saying."

Several minutes later there came into view a man pedaling a children's stern-wheel boat, the kind she'd played on during summer camps at Cloud Lake. This particular boat, done up in bright yellows and reds, had a smiling fiberglass Mickey Mouse standing behind the seat as a Venice gondolier. The driver's right cheek was swollen with an ugly purple bruise. His unblinking eyes seemed to register nothing. He pedaled hard on the bicycle-style gears in catatonic determination, heading not for shore but down the coast. The paddle wheel behind him churned a wide wake.

"Hello, excuse me," Sarah called out to him as she spilled air out of the sail.

He jerked his head up in surprise and stopped pedaling.

"Meulaboh. Which way is Meulaboh?"

He pointed in the direction he was heading. "Sixty kilometer."

"God, that far? I need to find a doctor for my brother."

He pointed behind him to the coastal hills. "Calang has military doctor. You go there." He bent his head and resumed his determined pedaling.

Sarah glanced back at the Calang hills. What, about fifteen miles away? And upwind, too. She tried tacking back and forth but didn't seem to get any closer. The breeze stiffened, furring the sea with small whitecaps. After an hour she figured that it would be easier just to land the boat on the beach and start walking.

Sarah set the sail again and steered for a gap in the head-high surf. The contrary wind, though, pushed the boat to where the waves were the biggest, thumping onto the sand. The woman cried out in alarm. "Hang on!" Sarah yelled as a wave built up behind them. The boat surfed down the face. The nose dug underwater, and the stern flipped high into the air, throwing Sarah overboard. The last thing she saw before she hit the water was Peter's head bobbing on the foam, and the hull of the boat falling upside down on top of him.

Chapter 15

When he reached the top of the beach, Ruslan stopped screaming. He forced himself to turn around. The wave that had frightened him swished a few feet up the sand. Just a normal wave, the kind he used to enjoy playing in.

Nonetheless, as he trudged toward Calang, he stayed on the landward side of sandy ridges as much as he could to keep the unsettling ocean from sight. He wondered if he'd ever be able to trust the sea again.

The land was silent. No birds whistled, no goats bleated, no children shouted, no horns honked, not a single mosque summoned the faithful to prayer. Caught in a leafless thornbush on one ridge was a sheet of yellowed newspaper. A corner of the sheet fluttered in the breeze, the crackle of paper unnaturally loud in the silence of this dead land. Ruslan picked it up. It was the front page of a Banda Aceh newspaper, dated December 25. He calculated on his fingers—it was the day before the flood. He scanned the headlines, which spoke of corruption in high places. How angry his father would get when reading such things. *Ruslan,* he'd say, *don't you ever forget, a poor man with honesty is richer than a thief with gold.* But the headlines' events were now meaningless to Ruslan, and he fashioned a hat out of the sheet. In the shade of its brim, he drank half the water in the remaining bottle.

He was trying not to look at the sea, but a curious sight caught his attention. In the distance ahead of him, a hundred yards offshore, a man pedaled a strange-looking boat, its sunshiny colors vibrant against the mottled water. One of those fiberglass stern-wheeler paddleboats from the Calang water park, where his father had taken him several times as a boy. It seemed an odd form of transport, but then again, why not? Probably easier than plodding through soft sand.

He lowered his head and kept walking, picking a path behind a wall of flattened weed that bordered drowned rice fields, newly planted green shoots turning brown. He came to another flattened village. For several minutes he studied the area from behind a stout tree that had survived the wave. When he saw no rebels foraging through the rubble, he moved forward. He forded several streams and had to swim partway across a wide estuary. When had he eaten last? The tangerines, and before that, Ibu Ramly's banana fritters. How delicious those fritters had been. How he'd love to have some now. Just one. Just a bite of one. The remembered taste of that filled his mind as he kept walking, walking, walking. The hills of Calang didn't seem to get any closer.

Cresting a sand hill, he saw a small fishing boat with a blue plastic sail tacking back and forth. He kept an eye on it as he walked. An inexpert sailor at the helm, that was for sure. Whitecaps from the stiffening sea breeze slapped the small hull. The sailor turned around and headed for shore, where the beach came to a small point, catching the bigger waves.

"Not there," Ruslan said, "not there!"

But the boat didn't change course. A big wave rose up behind the boat. That irrational panic seized him again, urging him away from the sea, but he could see what was going to happen, and he forced himself to sprint down to the point. The wave tipped the boat, catapulting the stern. Three people and a cat flew out of the hull. The orange cat and the white boy and white girl were in the air for only a second, but Ruslan recognized them at once. He had no time to wonder what they were doing here. Racing into the rushing wave, he first picked up the blob of orange washing past his thighs and threw the cat as far as he could onto the beach. An Acehnese woman in a head-dress bounced toward the shore. The white girl struggled to get to her feet. He grabbed her arm to help her, but she jerked free, fighting through the swirling foam to the overturned boat.

"Peter!" she yelled. "Peter!"

The boy hadn't come up. The girl tried to right the hull, but the next wave sent the boat crashing into her, and she lost her balance. Ruslan grabbed the edge of the hull and lifted it. The boy pushed out from underneath, spluttering and crying. Ruslan dragged him up to the beach and plopped him onto a piece of broken bamboo matting. The white girl raced up and grabbed her brother. "God, Peter, are you all right?"

He was coughing and crying. "I don't ever want to be on a boat again, I don't ever want to swim again, I want to go home, I want Mom and Dad, I want to go home, please, I want to go home."

The girl hugged him.

He stopped crying with a loud sniffle. "Where's Surf Cat?"

The cat was licking its belly. Ruslan picked it up and gave it to the boy.

"Thank you," the boy said.

The girl looked at him then with her blue eyes, the color fracturing the light. "Yes, thank you."

Ruslan waited for her to recognize him, but she didn't. His disappointment seemed outsized. What did it matter? Besides, the few minutes she'd been at the café she'd been fighting with her mother, not paying attention to who was serving the cold Cokes.

The Acehnese woman who'd been in the boat held her wet headdress tight under her chin with clenched fists, gazing out at the sea with a thousand-yard stare.

Green coconuts bobbed in the water, the swish of waves rolling a couple onto the sand. Ruslan chucked them higher onto the beach and waded out to get the others.

The woman broke out of her trance and called out in Acehnese, "There was a machete on the boat, but I suppose it's lost now."

The thought of the delicious meat in the coconuts made Ruslan light-headed with hunger. After taking off his shoes, he waded out to where the boat had tipped over, feeling the sand with his toes. Waves smashed into his chest. He knew this was a futile effort, that the chances of finding the machete were next to nothing, so perhaps that was why on the next step he felt the flat blade. He ducked into the water and plucked it, waving it triumphantly in the air.

Back onshore, he began hacking open a coconut. The woman grabbed the machete away from him. "You city boys are useless."

"How do you know I'm a city boy?"

"By the way you cut a coconut." Within seconds she handed him the sliced coconut, the exposed shell neatly holed. Ruslan's mouth watered and his throat convulsed, but he took the coconut to the girl.

The girl first let her brother drink. He guzzled and then turned his head away. She finished the rest. The woman whacked open the nut, making a scoop spoon out of discarded husk, and the girl slurped at the soft white meat.

The woman opened two more nuts, one for Ruslan and one for herself. "I hope you at least know how to climb a coconut tree," she said. "We'll need more." She put down the machete and said, "Where were you when it happened?"

Ruslan didn't have to ask what she meant. "Meulaboh."

"Me too. I'd gone to the market." She opened her mouth to say more but then squeezed her lips shut and lowered her head, pressing the crook of her trembling arm to her eyes.

Ruslan sat a distance away to give the woman her privacy and ate his coconut, forcing himself to take slow, measured scoops, wasting not a single delicious bit of it.

"Hello, excuse me," the girl called out to him. "My brother is sick. He needs a doctor. I need to go to Calang for a doctor." The girl spoke slowly and loudly, her tone capitalizing each word.

"That's where I'm going myself," Ruslan said.

The girl blinked. It seemed almost like magic, the way those blue eyes vanished and reappeared again. "You speak English?"

"Yes." Again he waited for her to recognize him—after all, how many employees in Meulaboh harbor-front cafés spoke English?

"Great. You can help me. What's your name?"

She still didn't place him. "My name is Ruslan." He didn't tell her that he'd served her family cold Cokes at the harbor, didn't tell her that his father had fixed their engine, didn't want his disappointment to deepen.

"Mine's Sarah. He's Peter."

What had happened to their mother and father?

But that he could imagine quite clearly, the sailboat taken by the flooding sea, the children becoming separated from the parents.

The girl Sarah rose to her feet. "We'd better get going, then."

The going was slow. Here the beach had sunk under the sea, which now lapped against swamps and toppled oil palms they had to navigate. Ruslan and the woman, whose name was Aisyah, took turns helping the fevered boy, whose main concern was his cat. Matter of fact, it seemed to be the cat who found the easiest traverses. At one point Aisyah muttered to Ruslan, "I think the creature's actually a djinn."

An hour before sunset it was Aisyah, and not the cat, who pointed out a grove of coconut palms several hundred yards inland. "We need some of those nuts," she said. "And we might as well spend the night."

They made what camp they could, using a torn piece of tarp they found in the grove for both ground cloth and roofing. Ruslan tucked the machete in the back of his jeans and wandered out of sight. Each village had men who specialized in climbing coconut trees to harvest nuts—pilots, they were called, because they were always up in the air—and he knew many boys who could do the same, but he'd never climbed a palm tree in his life. He didn't want to embarrass himself in front of the others.

Still, he managed, even though he slipped twice, scraping his arms. He whacked a couple of clusters out of the first palm, the nuts thudding on the ground. High on the second palm, a swarm of biting ants attacked him. Not wanting to climb a third tree, he gritted his teeth and chopped down the first cluster.

He was just raising the machete for another chop when he heard Sarah screaming.

Chapter 16

While Ruslan went in search of coconuts, Sarah went to find a secluded place to go to the bathroom. On her way back she momentarily lost her way and came across a well with a plastic bucket still attached to a rope tied to a wooden beam. She tested the well water. Salty but clean. Sarah looked around. Nobody was in sight. She stripped down to her bikini bottoms to give herself and her clothes a good soak.

She first washed the clothes, stomping on them with her feet to try to clean them of the dirt and mud. After draping them on the cement lip of the well, she hoisted up a bucket of water and poured it over her head. The cold delicious rush of it on her sunburned skin made her shiver. After several more buckets she put on her wet clothes, thinking wistfully of the dry clothes back home in her closet that she hardly ever wore. She had just tugged on her T-shirt when she noticed, out of the corner of her eye, shadows moving furtively among the palm trunks. Moving toward her. She instinctively screamed.

Ruslan charged in from out of nowhere with a yell, his machete raised. Two men had emerged from the palms. One of the men yelled something back at him. He stopped and lowered the machete. After an exchange with the men, he said to Sarah, "It's okay. They didn't mean to scare you. They are looking for help."

"Oh. Sorry." She noticed that the two young men were twins, identical down to the fuzzy mustaches they were trying to grow.

The twins joined the camp. Sarah's damp clothes chafed her, but that was nothing compared to her aching muscles and cuts. She and Aisyah coaxed Peter into swallowing a few mouthfuls of coconut. Then there was nothing else for them to do but try to sleep and wait for morning. Peter fidgeted with constant coughing. His hot, dry skin felt like paper.

Ruslan said something to Aisyah, who nodded, and he slipped out into the night.

Where was Ruslan going? In the constant, step-by-step struggle to make progress to the doctor at Calang, Sarah hadn't given him much thought. But he'd been there to help rescue Peter from the surf, and he'd rushed in with the machete when the two strangers had appeared. His absence now made her worry. She didn't feel as safe.

A minute later, though, he returned with a bucket of water. Aisyah tore part of her headdress into a handkerchief and dipped it into the water. She placed the wet cloth over Peter's forehead.

"Thank you," Sarah said, reaching for the cloth. "But let me do that."

Aisyah gently pushed her hand away and said something, which Ruslan translated. "She says you need your sleep. It's going to be a long walk tomorrow."

Ruslan's voice came across a vacuum. Sarah's mind seemed to be bubble-wrapped with fatigue. The tsunami had happened to another girl. She was just a hollow copy. She'd sleep for an hour and then wake up to take her turn nursing Peter.

When she did wake, it was dawn. Peter seemed to be sleeping deeply, although his breathing was wheezy and he was still hot to the touch. Ruslan and the twins were outside the tarp tent, murmuring their prayers, kneeling, and bowing on the ground.

What good would prayers do? If she got on her knees and prayed, would an angel appear and touch Peter's brow to make him better? Or maybe say, *I have a surprise,* and then their mother would walk in?

Her mother—her own mother—was dead. Odd how she still felt nothing.

Aisyah ducked under the tarp, with Surf Cat at her heels. She held a twisted white root the length of her palm. She washed it and ground half of it up between two rocks, then mixed the ground root into some coconut milk.

"It's *jamu* for Peter," Ruslan said. "Jamu is traditional medicine. This is for fever. She says the cat led her to the plant. She thinks the cat is a, what do you say, a devil."

Peter's eyes flew open and he sat upright. "Surf Cat is not a devil."

Ruslan lifted a hand. "No, no, not a bad devil. We call it a djinn."

"Genie," Sarah said. She stroked Surf Cat's fur. "He is a little strange."

Peter scowled. "He is not."

That scowl cheered Sarah. Some of her old brother was still there.

The band started hiking again. An hour later, with the blue sky already exuding an oven's heat, they came to the remains of a fishing village. A man squatted on his haunches in the middle of one foundation, idly scratching in the bare cement with a rusty nail. He glanced up at the passing group, watched for a second with a deadened expression, not even registering surprise at the sight of two Western children, and then threw the nail away to join them without a word.

Other survivors joined them. A middle-aged man with lopsided glasses, one of the frame's earpieces having snapped off. A woman and her elderly but wiry mother. Two more men, with one of the men's sons, who looked hardly any older than Ruslan but already wore a wedding ring. Another girl wearing shorts and a dirty towel over her shoulders to cover her budding breasts. She appeared oblivious to most everything, never speaking a word. Whenever the band paused, she squatted and pulled the towel over her head as though to hide herself. The middle-aged man, who carried himself with professorial dignity despite his lopsided glasses, and whom the others respectfully addressed as Bapak, shook his head and said to Sarah, "Mama, Bapa, family, *semua habis*." His hands translated: all gone.

Later it would seem to Sarah that these survivors had all joined at the same time, but in fact, they drifted in over the course of that day and the next. She couldn't remember when exactly. Except for the mute girl. She was the last, appearing out of a swamp toward the middle of the second day.

Those two days were a blur of swamps and sunken beaches and drowned oil palm plantations. The struggle of each hour, to get around or over or through some obstacle, seemed identical to any other hour. Ruslan and the others, including the tiny but strong grandmother, took turns helping Peter. The hills of Calang never seemed to get closer.

The second night they made camp in the ruins of a seashore mosque. Aisyah ground up the remaining half of the root and gave Peter a second dose of the *jamu*. He seemed to be holding his own—at least his fever and his cough weren't getting worse. Maybe the root did help, even if it wasn't real medicine.

By that time, Sarah was starting to think that perhaps Calang had been destroyed like everything else around them. There were those hills, though, with visible tree lines. The man in that paddleboat had seemed confident there was a doctor. The hospital had to be on one of the hills. She asked Ruslan about this before she went to sleep. He was lying on his back, staring up at the stars.

"Probably," Ruslan said, still gazing up at the

stars. "I don't know Calang very well. I'm not really going there, but to a village in the hills, where my father is."

"And the rest of your family?" Sarah asked delicately.

"No brothers or sisters. My mother died when I was little." Ruslan frowned in thought. "Maybe I am lucky."

Sarah understood the horrible logic of that, although she sensed a certain bewildered ache in his words, that he should have had no mother at all. "My mom drowned in the tsunami."

He turned his head to look at her. "I'm sorry," he said, with honest simplicity. And then, "The tsu-what?"

"The tsunami. It's a Japanese word for the big waves caused by earthquakes."

Ruslan was silent for a moment. "Is that what it was?"

"What did you think it was?"

He rose up on his elbow. "An Imam said God's punishment was coming."

"It was an earthquake, Ruslan."

A longer silence. "They didn't teach this at school."

"I didn't know what it was either at first."

Ruslan slowly nodded. "Your father?"

The question provoked a sharp anxiety. *Dad, be safe. Hang on.* "He's okay, except he broke his leg running from the wave. I had to leave him on Tiger Island to find my brother a doctor. You think they can organize a search party from Calang?"

"I'm sure they can," Ruslan said.

Sarah did not allow herself to doubt Ruslan's reassuring answer. Of course they would.

On the morning of the third day, the swamps at last gave way to higher ground, much of it planted with rice fields, now destroyed. The band made quick progress along remaining footpaths through the fields. The hills of Calang grew larger, and Sarah's hopes grew as well, only to be dashed when they came to an estuary and swamp too wide to ford. They would have to detour inland around it, adding another night to their trek.

Toward sunset, as they approached a small knob of ground upon which a farmer had built a shack, a faint drone sifted into the dull quiet. Sarah looked up and saw a dark speck low against the reddening clouds. A small aircraft, with a single engine and fixed wheels. The plane held a low and steady course just off the shoreline, but then abruptly banked and headed for the small band of survivors. It circled above them, descending lower with each circuit until it roared a hundred feet overhead. Framed in the open side door was a photographer, his blond ponytail whipping about in the wind as he aimed his camera at them.

"Help us!" Sarah screamed, waving her own arms. "Get us out of here!"

The photographer waved back. He lobbed something out of the plane that winked brightly as it fell to the ground a hundred feet away, landing by a goat dead on its side, legs stiff in the air. Sarah raced over to the object.

It was an almond and cranberry trail mix bar, looking as though it had come straight from a supermarket shelf. Sarah's mouth salivated. She tore open the wrapper with her teeth, the honeyed scent making her swoon. She was about to take the first wonderful bite when she stopped.

Don't be so selfish, she could hear her mother say. One of her constant annoying mantras.

Still, Sarah had the distinct and uneasy feeling that right at this moment her life was somehow in the balance. She could eat the trail bar, true, but afterward she'd forever be a certain kind of Sarah.

Nonsense, a sly voice said.

True, it was nonsense. Nonetheless, she broke the trail bar and gave Peter one of the halves.

The other she offered to the silent girl.

The girl sniffed it, nibbled a corner, and then crammed the whole of it into her mouth.

Bapak adjusted his glasses on his nose and scolded her, clearly telling the girl to thank Sarah.

"That's okay," Sarah said. She wished she had another bar to share. Maybe be like Jesus with the bread and fishes, multiplying the trail mix until everybody had enough to eat.

They climbed the thirty-foot-high hillock, rising neat as a button from the flat fields. Its lower slopes had been planted with corn, the plants ruined by the tsunami. The hut was nothing more than a thatched roof on crooked poles, with a rickety bamboo platform to rest upon. A stacked metal container held an untouched meal of moldy rice and greenish chicken legs. On the platform was an old shortwave radio. Bapak turned it on, and a voice crackled from the speaker, speaking a language Sarah didn't understand. The others gathered around to listen.

Ruslan stood separate from the others, staring at the distant foothills.

The way he was looking at them, Sarah became anxious. "You'll help us find that doctor, won't you?" she asked him. "I mean, what if he doesn't speak English?"

Ruslan turned and looked at her. The low sunlight threw his cheeks into high relief. And his eyes—she hadn't really noticed before how deep and clear they were. "Most doctors have some English," he said.

"But you'll help us?"

His lips pressed together for a moment and then he smiled, those eyes widening, light sparkling at the bottom of those black irises. "We're helping each other."

That reassured her.

After a quick meal of coconut, Bapak discussed something with the others and then spoke to Sarah. Ruslan interpreted, gesturing at the bamboo platform. "You and your brother can have the bed."

"No, no," Sarah said, and put her hand on the grandmother's shoulder. "Let her have it."

The grandmother scolded her. The bed was Sarah's. Sarah knew that the only way she could repay this touching kindness was to accept it.

"Thank you," she said.

Aisyah picked Peter up and laid him down on the bamboo slats.

"How you doing, champ?" Sarah asked him.

"Okay," he said, but the deepened flush of his skin and the listless, fevered look in his eyes told Sarah the truth. She kept her sense of helplessness at bay by thinking of the doctor at Calang. "We'll get you there tomorrow," she said.

Sarah asked if she could borrow the radio.

She spun the dial until she found an English news program. She learned then that the deadly tsunami had struck as far away as Thailand and India. Some commentators added their concerns about potential epidemics. One woman spoke of another danger, that of criminals presenting themselves as relief workers in order to abduct young orphans to sell elsewhere.

The silent girl approached out of the night shadows and sat beside her.

Sarah combed her matted hair with her fingers, working out the worst of the tangles. The girl slumped forward, sound asleep. Sarah put her down on the mat beside Peter and lay on the hard dirt floor, overcome with exhaustion herself.

Peter was restless and coughing. His fever seemed to be climbing. Aisyah had no more of the root to give him. She stroked his head and sang a lullaby.

> *Bungong jeumpa*
> *Bungong jeumpa,*
> *Meugah di Aceh . . .*

The sweetness of it was nearly unbearable. Worry for her father returned with a piercing vengeance. And her mother—but to her horror, her mother's face was a blank.

Chapter 17

Ruslan didn't sleep well that night on the farmer's hill. The evening's meal of coconut was sour in his stomach. By God, he was getting sick of the stuff. He didn't want to eat another coconut in his whole life.

But that wasn't what was really bothering him. Sarah had asked him to go with her and Peter into Calang. He didn't want to. He should start heading into the green hills to Ie Mameh. Bapak and Aisyah could help Sarah and Peter.

Sometime in the morning he would say his good-byes and veer off to the north, making his way on his own. He had his father to find. Surely Sarah would understand.

When the band descended the hillock at dawn, Ruslan led the way. He was eager to get to Ie Mameh. He was certain that by the end of the afternoon he'd be hugging his father, kissing his cheeks. The thought of it cheered him so much that he started whistling. As he jumped a small ditch, he noticed Sarah staring at him, and he fell silent, feeling guilty.

"No, no, don't stop," she said. "It's so good to hear somebody whistling."

He bowed to her and finished the tune.

"My dad could whistle," Sarah said. "He couldn't sing, though. It was torture to be with him in the car, him and Mom singing stupid love songs. Wasn't it, Peter?"

The twins had fashioned a stretcher from some scavenged bamboo and burlap and were carrying him. Surf Cat, too, was hitching a ride, snoozing by Peter's side. Peter smiled weakly. "Awful," he agreed.

Ruslan had no idea what Sarah's parents were like, but the image of them singing duets in a car made him grin. "Love songs?"

"Yeah, like this one." Sarah began to sing a song about feelings, feelings of love.

Ruslan winced exaggeratedly, pressing his hands to his ears. Sarah laughed and hit him lightly on the arm. It was the first time he'd heard her laugh. It was a nice sound, a normal sound, a sound from Ruslan's previous life, when the sea had still been steady. The small happiness of hearing it was like the sweet juice that broke each day of the Ramadan fast.

An hour later they came to a shallow place where they could ford the estuary and then backtrack to a road that led into Calang. Several miles to the right stretched the first of the green foothills. Ruslan stepped to the side, letting others pass, and stared at the valleys. Ie Mameh was on the slopes of one, but he couldn't remember which one. Well, there'd be other villages. He'd find out.

"What's wrong?" Sarah asked, startling him. He hadn't noticed her approach.

He pointed to the hills. "That's where my mother's village is. My father's there."

She frowned. He had to look away as she said, "You're not leaving us, are you? You promised me, Ruslan, you promised me you'd help me find the doctor."

He shook his head. "I didn't promise you."

"But you have to help us. Please. Peter's sicker this morning than last night."

"Sarah, I have to go find my father. Bapak and Aisyah will help you."

"We need you, Ruslan. We're foreigners here, nobody else speaks English, and Peter is sick, you have to help us. Please. Your father is okay, he'll be okay for a couple more days—"

Ruslan whirled on her. All the fear that he'd kept way down at the bottom of his heart broke to the surface. "How do you know he is okay? He is up there with the rebels. You are right. You are a foreigner. You don't know anything about this country. You don't know how dangerous that is. I have to go find him. I am *his son*."

He was aware of how his voice shook. He was aware too of how tears filled Sarah's eyes. They tore at him, but some duties were higher than all others. What did his father say? *A man's duty is first to God, and then to family, and then to those who ask for help.*

Sarah opened her mouth to speak, but before she said anything, the buzzing of a helicopter broke through the morning's silence. Her gaze snapped away as she stared over his shoulder. Ruslan turned to see a red helicopter zooming toward them. It banked around the hillock that the band had left earlier and headed toward them, slowing down to hover above a patch of broken road a hundred feet away. Ruslan's head throbbed with the roar of its blades and the piercing whine of its engine. Through the whirlwind of dust and dirt, he saw a white man in the passenger cabin point at Sarah.

The helicopter settled to the ground on its skids. Apart from some numbers and letters on the tail, the helicopter bore no markings. The man got out, scurrying over to Sarah in a crouch. A bigger man followed, his round belly jiggling.

"We come to get you," the first man shouted to Sarah over the helicopter's noise. His gaunt jaws held a dark shadow of beard.

"Your brother?" the fat man asked, with an even heavier accent, pointing at Peter in the stretcher. The man's small eyes peered out from underneath a thick brow scalded by sun.

"Who are you?" Sarah said suspiciously.

"United Nations," the second man said.

Ruslan frowned. United Nations? The man was lying. The government would never let the United Nations fly around Aceh so freely like this. He caught Sarah's eye and shook his head.

She asked, "Do you have any ID?"

The fat man grunted and turned to the other. They spoke briefly in a guttural language. "I am Hans and he is Iverson," the fat man said. "This is the emergency situation, we don't have our papers. Come now, the helicopter is waiting."

Sarah shook her head. "I don't know you."

"You must come with us," the first man said. "The rebels, they are here and they shall kidnap you."

The helicopter pilot made hurry-up gestures.

The fat man grabbed Peter from the stretcher.

"Let him go!" Sarah shrieked. She flew at the man and sank her teeth into his elbow. He roared with pain. Aisyah snatched Peter away and hugged him to her side.

Bapak raised the machete in a menacing gesture.

The skinny white man took a precautionary step backward. "There are rebels!" he shouted at Sarah. "It is dangerous! You shall come!"

The mute girl picked up a stone and threw it at the helicopter. The stone fell far short, but Ruslan and the others also picked up rocks and cocked their arms. The skinny man cursed, and he and his companion rushed back to the helicopter, which took off in a shrieking blast of air.

In the silence that backfilled the chopper's racket, Ruslan could see how Sarah trembled. She took several deep breaths and then gave the mute girl a hug. "The way you scared off the helicopter, that was something. Thank you."

The girl gravely nodded.

Ruslan chucked his rock aside and touched Sarah's arm. She glanced up at him. "Oh. Thanks for helping. Bye, hope you find your dad."

Ruslan smiled. "If we're going to Calang, we'd better not just stand here."

Her face was blank for a moment, and then joy rose into her blue eyes. "You're coming?"

"You're right. My father will be okay." Beneath his smile, Ruslan hoped so. But sometimes one's duty to God is exactly the same as one's duty to others. Especially, perhaps, to foreigners in one's country.

Chapter 18

What Sarah could see of Calang, about a mile away on the other side of destroyed fields, filled her with fresh worry. Apart from one white building sticking up like a lone tooth, the town appeared to be mostly rubble. Several big tents had been pitched on one of the hills, and a ramshackle camp of makeshift huts hunkered on the adjoining hill.

Several hundred yards away, in a former rice field, an orange excavator lurched and clanked, its scoop bucket digging a large pit in the ground. The sight of that partially reassured Sarah. At least somebody was doing something.

The rice field lay beside an asphalt road, which had been cleared to this point, debris bulldozed to the side. A dump truck barreled down the road from the town toward them, trailing a cloud of dust. In the corner of the rice field, a soldier with a rifle slung over his shoulder and a white mask wrapped around his face stood in the shade of a big tree. Paper and plastic from the tsunami still clung to the tree's lowest branches.

"Maybe he knows where the doctor is," Sarah said to Ruslan. "Could you ask?"

The dump truck turned off onto the rice field. Ruslan and Sarah waited until the dust cloud settled before approaching the soldier. His eyes were shadowed with fatigue, his green uniform streaked with filth. "*Salam*," Ruslan said respectfully. The soldier grunted a reply, staring at Sarah with eyes too exhausted to show curiosity. Ruslan spoke to him in the local language. The soldier replied, nodding at the hill with the tents.

"The clinic is behind the big green tent," Ruslan said.

Sarah closed her eyes. "Thank God," she murmured.

Aisyah shrieked.

Startled, Sarah twirled around. Aisyah and the others were staring at the truck, which had backed up to the large pit. Its dump bed tilted. Dozens of corpses tumbled into the pit, a jumble of bodies, arms and legs sticking out every which way. Smaller bodies of children settled into gaps. Several corpses were stuck on the lip of the truck's bed, blocked by a body in gray overalls that was hung up on something. The driver slammed the truck forward a few feet. This jolted the remaining bodies loose. The corpse in the overalls landed on the edge of the pit. The driver got out of the cab and pushed the body with his feet, rolling it over the side into the pit.

Sarah watched all this because she couldn't believe what she was seeing. Then she threw up on the side of the road. Aisyah did the same.

The dump truck growled back onto the road. The driver braked to a stop beside Sarah and said something around the roughly rolled cigarette smoldering in his lips.

"He's asking if we want a ride," Ruslan interpreted quietly. He looked pale and shaken.

Sarah shuddered at the thought. "No thanks, we'll walk."

Ruslan asked the driver a question, which the man answered with an indifferent shrug. He drove off with a wave of his cigarette, leaving a stinky smell of diesel exhaust and, underneath that, the sickly sweet smell of death.

"He told me they're burying the dead people before everyone else gets sick from disease," Ruslan said. He was quiet for several steps and then added, in a quieter and pained voice, "Nobody is saying the prayers of the dead for them. Nobody will even know who they are."

"That's terrible," Sarah murmured. She imagined a father running around frantically looking for his missing son. *Have you seen him, have you, where is he, he must be alive, I know he is alive, I must find him!* And his son one of the anonymous dead. Buried with a thousand others.

At least Sarah knew for sure her mother was dead. Knew where she was temporarily buried. How awful to be able to take comfort in knowing such things!

Ruslan swung his arms as though to loosen something off his back. "I thought maybe that dead man in the gray clothes was my father. My brain wanted to explode. But he was too big. Tattoos on his arms. And my father is in Ie Mameh."

Imagine that, happy that someone else's dead father wasn't one's own. But Sarah knew that she would feel the same. Perfectly understandable.

They came to the foot of the first big hill. Down the road, in one section of the flattened town, Sarah could see men with scarves around their faces and plastic bags around their hands picking through the wreckage, hauling corpses to the dump truck.

On the hill two soldiers emerged from a guard

post of broken planks roughly nailed together, and sauntered down to the band. They spoke with Bapak and Ruslan. There were a few minutes of argument and confusion. It was clear from the soldiers' gesturing that the men in the band were to immediately go to work helping gather the corpses, while the women were to go up to the camp on the adjacent hill. On its upper slopes was a clutch of huts made of salvaged cardboard, plastic, plywood, tin. Ruslan argued politely and firmly, pointing to Peter. In the end, the twins weren't allowed to carry the stretcher to the clinic. Sarah and Ruslan had to do it themselves. One of the soldiers herded Aisyah and the other women away before Sarah even had a chance to thank them.

The collection of tents had been hastily erected on the dusty slope between stands of scraggly trees and brush. One stiff wind would probably blow the tents away. Sarah noticed a big green tent with a wooden sign out front that had a military-looking shield painted on it. Stern black letters announced the tent to be a command post of some kind. A man in civilian clothes, his hair cut flat to his scalp, stood in front of the flap door, brooding over the ruined town. He swung his hooded gaze to Ruslan and Sarah, carrying the stretcher. Ruslan, at the front, picked up his pace.

When they turned the corner, Sarah whispered, "Who was that?"

"I don't know," Ruslan said shortly.

The brown clinic tent, with Red Cross and Red Crescent signs painted on the thin canvas, tilted to one side as though a breeze had already tried to snatch it. The front desk at the clear plastic doorway looked as though it had been scavenged from a grade school. Behind it sat a young man in army trousers and a dirty T-shirt. He shook his head and said something. Sarah guessed he was saying that there was no more room.

Ruslan spoke quickly. Sarah caught the word "tourist" and *tamu*, a local word that she knew meant "guest."

The man sighed and waved them inside.

"We'll have to find room for Peter," Ruslan said to Sarah.

Two dozen cots and another dozen makeshift ones crammed the hot tent. Patients lay on them in dull apathy. Many had broken bones, but only several of these bones had been set with plaster. The other limbs had been set with sticks and tape, or simply wrapped in cloth. A number of patients were children, like Peter, and like him, many were feverish and coughing. Ruslan found a space in the back of the tent beneath an open flap that caught a draft of breeze. They put down the stretcher.

Peter moaned and opened his eyes. "Where are

we? It's hot." After a racking cough, he peered up at the slope of canvas above him, propped up by large aluminum poles. "What's that? Why's there something over my head?"

Sarah knelt by him. "It's a tent, silly. We're in a clinic. And here comes a nurse."

The dark circles under the nurse's eyes looked like they were etched onto her cheekbones. She asked for Peter's name and age, which she wrote down with a pencil stub in a ragged notebook. She took his temperature with an old-fashioned mercury thermometer and felt his pulse, which she noted.

"Where's the doctor?" Sarah asked.

The nurse shook her head in irritation. Ruslan repeated the question in the local language. The nurse snapped at him. Ruslan said to Sarah, "He's worked for forty-eight straight hours and he's having a rest. He'll be here soon."

The nurse gave Ruslan an enamel basin half-filled with murky water and a cloth. Sarah dipped the cloth and washed Peter's dirty chest, his ribs starting to stand out like toothpicks. She was losing weight herself. Before, her shorts had pinched a little. Now they hung on her hips. On the trek early that morning she'd found some rope and had made a belt for them. Maybe when she got home she could write a diet book. Take one tsunami. Add coconuts.

She could hear her mother. *Nothing to joke about.*

True.

She washed Peter's cheeks and became aware of Ruslan's gaze. He was watching her with an odd intensity that flustered her. "What?" she said lightly. "Am I drooling or something?"

"Peter is very lucky to have a sister like you."

She could feel pink spots blossom on her cheeks. The last time she'd felt this pleased was when her dad had complimented her on her parallel parking. He'd been teaching her in the family car. Just a month ago. Back in her other life, before the ocean had destroyed it. What had he said? *A girl who can parallel park like that can go places in life. Why, just think, you could even be a garage's chief parking attendant.* She had given him a mock scowl and punched his shoulder. And was smiling now at the memory.

But the truth about her and Peter was unavoidable. Her smile died. "I really haven't been such a great sister. We could fight. I could be mean." She looked at Ruslan, at his soft black eyes. They drew something out of her she'd never ever spoken about, not even to her dad. "My mother loved Peter a lot more than me."

Ruslan shook his head. "I never had a mother,

but still, I think mothers are mothers. They love their children all the same."

"In theory. Not in reality. My mother never wanted me. I was a mistake. A pregnancy at the wrong time." Sarah dipped the cloth into the bowl. "My mother's last thing, the last thing she did, just as the tsunami was starting to come in, she slapped me across the face and yelled at me to help Peter instead of my dad with his broken leg."

She could still feel the blow. Could see her mother's icy look. She squeezed the cloth hard. Emotions whirled in her like a slot machine gone crazy. Then they came to an instant stop, but all mixed up and unreadable. Tears sprang to her eyes. "Peter would have been okay," she said. The words came out hot and hard, burning her throat. "He was running. I could have helped Mom get Dad up the hill in time. We would all have been okay."

She hurled the cloth, not seeing the man sidling toward them through the cots. The cloth smacked him in the face. He picked it off and dropped it to the side. It was the man from the green tent. His yellowed eyes were as cold as dirty ice cubes. He pointed a finger at her. "You," he said, the simple English word heavily accented. "Come with me."

Chapter 19

The man wore civilian clothes, the neatest and cleanest trousers and shirt that Ruslan had seen in days, but his flat-cut hair and flatter gaze told Ruslan who he was. Military intelligence. He had the bearing of a senior officer.

Ruslan and Sarah followed him to the big green tent. In a stifling corner of the tent, the man ordered Sarah to sit on the single stool in front of a plywood sheet that served as his desk. Ruslan stood to the side.

"I'm sorry," Sarah said. "I didn't mean to hit you. I didn't see you."

"No problem," the intelligence officer said in English. He seemed to be softening up to her. In fact, all he wanted to know was why a Westerner would be in the clinic. Ruslan interpreted for the both of them, relaying the officer's questions, giving him Sarah's answers.

"My dad's still on Tiger Island," Sarah said. "Can you organize a search party for him?"

The man extracted a half-smoked cigarette from his shirt pocket. He held it up. "More precious than gold right now," he told Ruslan, speaking in Acehnese, although he wasn't from the province. The refined features of his face suggested he was a Javanese. He lit the cigarette with a lighter and took a deep and reverent swallow of smoke. He carefully pinched out the cigarette and tucked it back into his shirt pocket. "She wants a rescue party? Does she know how many people are missing? We don't have enough people to bury the dead, let alone go searching for the missing."

Ruslan nodded and turned to translate for Sarah. She looked at him with expectant eyes. "He will try," Ruslan said. "He will do his best."

She exhaled in relief. "Thank you." She reached over the plywood desk to shake the officer's hand. "Thank you so much. My dad is pretty tall—" She stopped and snorted. "God, what am I saying? You won't be able to miss him. The only tall white man on the island, hobbling around on a broken leg. He can start fires with just sticks, like a real caveman, so look for smoke and stuff. I'd like to go with you, but I should stay with my brother. Um, can I go back to Peter now?"

The officer shooed her away with a friendly gesture.

After she'd darted out of the tent, the man said to Ruslan, "So I will try, will I?"

"Shouldn't you?"

"How? Phone lines, power lines, radio, everything down, all the roads cut. We're our own world here." He shook his head and chuckled without humor. "Typical Western arrogance. Think we ought to drop everything to go look for one of their own. Do Westerners deserve something special that we don't?"

Ruslan looked down at the plywood, warped from water. "She's alone with her sick brother and is very brave."

A grunt, then in a softer voice, "Those blue eyes. I knew several people in Lamno and the hill villages around there with blue eyes. Portuguese ancestors. Every once in a while a kid's born with blue eyes."

"May I go now?"

"Your mother had blue eyes. Not as blue as this girl Sarah, but blue enough."

Ruslan forced himself to keep his head bent. He manufactured a puzzled frown before lifting his gaze to the man's coldly amused one. "What are you talking about?"

"Not that I ever met her. Your father told me. We had a few talks, your father and I."

The man was military intelligence. He must have been one of the officers who'd interrogated his father over the years. Still, it was safest to play dumb. "I don't know what you're talking about."

"Yusuf the mechanic. I suppose you're on your way to Ie Mameh to join him, are you? Come up all the way from Meulaboh?"

"I'm helping Sarah," Ruslan said stiffly.

The man's half smile disappeared. "You'll have to do body-gathering detail before you can get your rations. Commandant's regulations. That's me. Temporary commandant, like everything around here. The officers had the best quarters, the ones on the beach. They all drowned. Many of the enlisted men, too. I'll assign you to the central sector. By the gasoline pumps." He called over one of the soldiers and told him to take Ruslan down to his assigned sector. As Ruslan left the tent, the temporary commandant called out, "Make sure you do a good job. Lots of smashed-up cars around that area. Remember to look inside them. Don't want to miss anybody." That amused half smile was back on his face, back in his voice.

The bulldozer had cleared a road all the way to the ruined Pertamina fuel station. A private in charge of the corpse-gathering detail told Ruslan to find a rag to cover his mouth and plastic bags to put on his hands. A bearded man in a filthy robe worked with this particular crew. Even clerics weren't being spared this gruesome task.

The stink of death clogged the air. Ruslan breathed shallowly through his mouth. He found a clean cloth, the flag of a local sports club somehow still flying on a short pole. Plastic bags were everywhere in the rubble. He picked out two of the cleanest ones. As he did so, he kept glancing up at the range of distant green hills. He'd have to sneak out of town sometime in the night. The cleric would know where Ie Mameh was—they were always going off and preaching at various towns and villages.

The cleric and a man who had the pudgy appearance of a wealthy merchant slung a body onto the back of the truck. Ruslan joined them. He murmured to the cleric, "Excuse me, sir, do you know where Ie Mameh is? I know it's up in the hills there, but I don't know where exactly."

Bits of leaves and dirt stuck to the cleric's beard. He peered at Ruslan as though looking at another Ruslan underneath the outer one. "What do you want there with those rebels, boy? Has not God punished us for our warmongering?"

"Get to work!" the private shouted at them.

This area was still richly veined with bodies. Ruslan's gaze wandered past crumpled adults to the small, fly-covered form of a toddler upon a wash of fine gray sand. He would retrieve her first. As he bent to pick her up, he noticed that crabs had eaten her eyes.

He threw up.

The private laughed.

Ruslan wiped his mouth, glowering at the private. "Why don't you help?"

"Let's make sure you're completely emptied out," the private said, and slammed the butt of his rifle into Ruslan's stomach.

Ruslan doubled over, gasping for breath.

The merchant whispered, "You dumb boy, don't you know not to talk back to them?"

Another soldier, one with an additional stripe, had seen the private's assault. He said quietly to Ruslan, "My men are just as traumatized as anyone. They've lost many comrades."

After that, Ruslan kept silent. He and the

others gathered bodies, carting them off to the truck to be unceremoniously dumped on top of other corpses. His mind retreated to a corner, and his senses became dulled to the crabs and flies, the greenish abdomens, the mottled skin that often slipped in his grasp, the rising smell, the stirrings of maggots.

Whenever he or another found a holy Qur'an, pages damply plastered together, the book would be put on a high place in the sun, upon a hedge, a remnant of wall. Beside a pile of sodden fabric that might once have been curtains, Ruslan spotted a drawing pad, open to a sketch of a horse. A heavy, childish hand, much erasing, no talent, but done with enthusiasm. Beside the book was a box of crayons. He put the drawing and the box on top of an overturned car, wondering as he did so if he would ever draw again in his life. Art seemed such an insignificant thing, a part of his life that had been swept away for good.

Make sure you look inside the cars, the intelligence officer had said. Ruslan peered inside the overturned sedan. Empty.

A minute later he found a brass plaque engraved with the Bismillah, the graceful Arabic proclaiming Allah's compassion and mercy. He picked up the plaque and studied it before propping it beside a

Qur'an. The slaughter made no sense, but who was he to question God, who was not only the Merciful and Compassionate, but also the Destroyer and the Killer?

Together with a young man who might have been a schoolteacher, Ruslan hauled the body of a man in business clothes to the truck. Who had this man been? Had he been a liar and a thief? A good and faithful Muslim? A loving husband and father? A wife beater?

"A cubic meter of water weighs one ton," the young man said as though he were in a classroom. "A column of water one meter square and twenty meters high weighs twenty tons. If the water came in at forty kilometers an hour, the force would be . . ." He droned on and on, calculating the mathematics of death.

The corpse gatherers entered one of the few buildings that still had a second floor, although much of the roof had collapsed. A woman was trapped in a small prayer room on the second floor. Perhaps she'd been praying and giving thanks for surviving the earthquake, reciting from the gilded Qur'an near her hand. A gold band glinted on her soft and well-manicured finger. Perhaps she'd been a new bride. Ruslan lifted the roof beam that had fallen across her head, soft black hair poking out from underneath her headdress. Her eyes were partially open. Light blue irises peered unseeingly at him. She looked fresher than the other bodies he'd gathered, her skin firm and taut.

And even a bit warm to the touch.

A horrible understanding dawned—she had just recently died. Perhaps only minutes ago.

He squeezed his eyes shut and took several deep breaths. When he opened his eyes, the Qur'an by her hand swam into focus. He picked it up, weighed it for a second, and then hurled it to the ground.

The others near him stopped and stared. The schoolteacher stepped back, as though God were about to fling a bolt down from the heavens.

"Now, young brother," the merchant said, his voice uncertain.

"Why?" Ruslan said.

The merchant sighed. "An ancient question, old as man's first sorrow. Who can understand? The one thing we know for certain is that we are slaves to God's will. All we can do is submit and strive to become better Muslims."

Ruslan was aware of his scowl but unable to erase it.

"Do you think me a sermonizing hypocrite, young brother?" the merchant said. "I lost my wife and one of my children."

Shame drove Ruslan's scowl away. Without another word he and the merchant lifted the woman onto a mat and others carried her to the waiting dump truck.

He was thinking about that woman, and regretting that no one would be saying the prayer of the dead for her, when he turned a corner that the bulldozer had recently plowed, pushing off a chain of cars blocking the way.

And there, on its side ten feet in front of him, its blue and white sides badly battered and its windows smashed, was an ancient Ford.

His father's car.

Chapter 20

The groans of the wounded and the coughs of the sick filled the clinic tent. A mother stood by a cot, using a piece of cardboard to fan her small daughter's face. The girl's chest rose and fell with her struggling breaths. She was half-conscious and hadn't been able to eat the rice gruel her mother had tried to feed her.

A male nurse had just made the rounds with the food. Peter refused his bowl as well, turning his head away.

"You *have* to eat, okay?" Sarah kept bugging him until he'd swallowed a third. The rest she finished. Tasteless, but at least it quieted her growling stomach.

The female nurse made rounds after the meal, handing out a cup of water and medicine from a bottle.

When she got to Sarah, she carefully broke a white round pill, handing Sarah half. Sarah peered at the label on the bottle.

"Aspirin?" she said. "Half an aspirin? That's all my brother's getting? He needs antibiotics, for God's sake!"

The nurse shrugged. Not a callous shrug, just a very tired one, but Sarah jumped to her feet and thrust her face at the nurse. "Where's the doctor? I want to see the doctor."

"*Nanti*," the nurse said, and pushed by her.

"And you don't give aspirin to children!" Sarah shouted after her. "Everybody knows that!"

She slumped down by Peter's side. Surf Cat lifted his head and sniffed the half pill in her hand. "What do you think, Surf Cat?" she asked. "Is it okay to give Peter half an aspirin?"

Surf Cat stretched luxuriously before slipping through a broken seam in the tent.

Nanti, the nurse had said. Another local word that Sarah happened to know. Her father, studying an Indonesian phrase book, had made a comment about it. "*Nanti* means 'later,'" he had said. "In the Indonesian culture it has the same meaning as the

Spanish *mañana*, but without quite the same sense of urgency."

Sarah sniffed the cup of water. Smelled like wood smoke. Boiled. What harm could half an aspirin do to Peter? He wasn't a baby. It would help his temperature, at least. Might have a problem swallowing it, though. Sarah crushed the pill into powder, which she dissolved in the water before waking him, holding him up with an arm around his shoulder. He groggily took a sip and then said, "I was dreaming about Mom."

"That's nice," Sarah said. "Another sip, please. It's your medicine."

"Remember when she had Mr. Chouri over for dinner and a lot of the neighbors didn't come and he played that weird music of his and he taught Mom how to dance it?"

"Peter, finish drinking this, will you?"

He swallowed the rest of it and lay back down. "I dreamed she was dancing and dancing."

Sarah remembered that night. She knew more of the story than Peter. Mr. Chouri was an immigrant. There were ugly rumors about him that had made her parents angry. Her mother threw a party for him and invited all the people who were talking about him behind his back. Only a few came. But her mother and father had had a great old time, dancing to that strange music. Her mother had insisted that Sarah have a try, but she'd refused.

Another, more recent memory came to her, one she had tried her best never to think about. Early last summer, as she'd looked in the master bedroom closet for her mother's new black pumps to try on, she had found a box full of old diaries. She'd picked one out at random, the journal her mother kept the year she was born, and opened it.

Her mother's curly handwriting was branded into her memory.

My resentment of this child within me borders on hate. I don't want to have it. I don't love it and won't love it when it's born.

She had slammed the diary shut and shoved it back in its place, but it had been too late.

Maybe this was why she couldn't feel a thing for her own dead mother. Maybe the poison of what she wasn't supposed to know was turning her into an unfeeling monster.

"Hello."

She startled at the voice. A man, wearing glasses that magnified his weary, drooping eyes. He peered at the nurse's notepad.

Sarah stood with expectant hope. "You're the doctor?"

He nodded. "Dr. Azril." He crouched by Peter's

side and felt his forehead, then took his pulse and tapped his scrawny chest. Pressing one end of a cardboard tube to Peter's chest, he cocked his head and listened at the other end.

"Um, shouldn't you use a stethoscope?" Sarah asked uncertainly.

"No stethoscope. Hospital gone. Much destroyed." He gave her a tired but still friendly smile. "We use emergency technology."

He asked Sarah what had happened, and Sarah explained about the tsunami and how Peter had swallowed water.

"Yes, it is common," Dr. Azril said, gesturing to several of the other coughing patients.

"But you have medicine for him, right? Antibiotics and stuff to make him better?"

Dr. Azril sighed and stood. "No medicine. All gone. But we can pray, yes?"

Before Sarah could think of words to say, the woman tending to her daughter began a crescendo of wailing.

The girl lay still and quiet, no longer struggling to breathe.

Chapter 21

Ruslan gaped at the Ford, feeling as though his stomach had been sucker punched again.

What was his father's car doing here at Calang?

The intelligence officer's sly voice spoke into his ear. *I've had talks with your father,* he said. *Make sure you look inside the smashed-up cars for bodies,* he said.

Ruslan ran to the car and then halted several feet away. He didn't want to look. He couldn't look. He called to the merchant. "Can you see if anybody's inside?"

"What's the matter, son?"

"Please look."

The merchant peered through one of the

shattered windows. "Nobody." He frowned curiously at Ruslan. "You know this car?"

"My father's. It shouldn't be here. It should be in—" A memory sharp as a blade cut off Ruslan's voice. This morning, the first awful truckload of bodies being dumped into the mass grave. That body in the gray overalls . . . maybe those marks on the arms hadn't been tattoos but bruises. Perhaps the body had looked fatter than his father because dead bodies bloated.

The dump truck stood a hundred yards down the road, loaded up for another run. The driver was just getting into the cab. Ruslan sprinted and jumped up in the back as the driver started the engine. Ruslan crouched down by the awful cargo as the driver eased the clutch, the truck shaking and rattling in first gear. A gunshot rang out through the air, followed by the private's shouting. The truck halted, and the driver stuck his head out the window to yell, "What now?"

Ruslan yanked off his distinctive yellow shirt and stuffed it underneath a corpse. Then, with a queasy twist of his stomach, he wormed his way into the bodies on the truck bed, arranging the blue-eyed woman's arm so it lay across his head.

Revulsion and claustrophobia swamped him. He pressed his face to the bed's hard metal and hyperventilated with short little gasps. He was about to abandon this insane ploy and bolt out of the truck when something curious happened. The woman's arm, instead of being a dead weight, became a mother's encouraging embrace. *His* mother. He heard her voice: *Calm down, my love, calm down.*

His revulsion passed, a breeze swept away his claustrophobia, and his tumult quieted.

"Well, he isn't here," he could hear the driver saying in annoyance to the private, who was still breathing hard from his run. "I got a job to do, let me do it."

The truck bumped down the road and after a while slowed to a stop. The cab door opened. What was going on? This wasn't the grave site.

Above him the driver's breath rasped heavily. Ruslan tilted his chin and cracked his eyes. The truck had halted behind a screen of fallen trees, and the driver was kneeling by the woman's side. He reached for her hand to tug off the gold wedding ring. "You won't need that," he muttered.

An incandescent fury shot through Ruslan. He bolted upright and grabbed the man's throat. The driver screeched, his eyes bulging with terror. He yanked away from Ruslan's grip and fell backward off the truck, his head hitting the ground with a solid thud. He lay still in a limp heap.

Ruslan's anger was still with him. *Serves him right, the corpse robber.* Nonetheless, he checked the man's breathing and pulse. Satisfied the man would live, he tugged him into a patch of shade and then climbed up into the cab behind the driver's wheel. After some grinding of clutch and gears, he got the truck going and barreled down the road, swinging into the turnoff with a squeal of tires.

The excavator looked like a busy one-armed creature, hard at work making a second burial trench. The first hadn't yet been covered. A man was shoveling lime over the bodies.

Ruslan jumped out of the cab and ran to the edge of the grave, ignoring the lime shoveler's astonished stare. He walked around the lip of the hole, peering down at the horrible puzzle of dead bodies piled at random, their congealed mass lightly coated with lime, like sugar frosting. The corpse of the man in gray overalls was to the side of the pile, where it had rolled to a stop facedown at the bottom of the trench's steep slope. Ruslan slid down the side and turned the corpse's shoulders. A pockmarked face, the old acne scars clearly visible despite the skin's greenish bloat. Not his father.

"What the hell are you doing?" The guard stood at the edge of the grave, his rifle unslung, ready to use.

Not his father. Ruslan climbed back up in a daze. It was the most curious sensation, relief that wasn't relief. Just because this dead man in the gray overalls wasn't his father didn't mean that his father wasn't dead.

"The driver got sick," he told the guard. "I was assigned to replace him." He jumped into the back of the truck and picked up the young, blue-eyed woman. She felt light as air in his arms, even when he jumped off. He gently placed her on the ground and waved his arms at the excavator operator, who stopped the gears and leaned out the side of his cab. "Dig her a grave," he told the operator. "A private grave, away from the others, so we can mark it with something."

The guard slung his rifle over his shoulder. "A relative?" he asked sympathetically.

"Yes," Ruslan said. In his heart he added, *my mother*. His mother, who had died as young as this unknown woman. The mother he'd never known, except for one sweet second just minutes ago, when she had come to him to calm his terror.

He removed the woman's wedding ring, its inner circle inscribed with a date. He was sure that somebody would recognize the ring and have at least the mercy of knowing where a loved one was buried.

There had been no ritual washing of the body,

and there was no shroud, but in the truck's cab were several white T-shirts still in their plastic packages that the driver had no doubt looted. Ruslan put one on and tucked another around the woman as a symbol for all that was lacking. He said the prayer for the dead, the guard and excavator operator and lime sprinkler respectfully standing behind him.

When he was finished, he turned around. Two men in civilian clothes had appeared out of nowhere to join the impromptu mourning. One had a scarred arm, the other a dead white eye.

Chapter 22

Sarah pressed her hands against her ears to block out the mother's anguished crying.

Please, would somebody come take that woman away? Peter needs his peace and quiet.

No medicine for her sick brother.

After all she'd been through, pushing on and on and on to get Peter to a doctor.

Well, they'd found a doctor.

And the doctor couldn't do anything. Except tell her to pray.

Pray? Who was she going to pray to? A God who'd allowed thousands and thousands of people to die in the first place? That made no sense at all.

The doctor checked the girl and shook his head.

The nurse expertly wrapped the girl in a white sheet. She was probably real good at doing that by now. The mother, whose keening had muted to quiet sobbing, picked up the bundle and left the tent.

Sarah stood still for a moment and then ran out of the tent into the rich light of a golden afternoon. "Excuse me," she called out to the woman, who turned to her, the white bundle cradled in her arms. "I'm so sorry."

The woman stared blankly at Sarah for a moment with reddened eyes. She turned away without a word and walked stiffly on.

When Sarah returned to the hot shadows of the tent and Peter's side, Surf Cat was just slipping through the tent's ripped seam. The seam tugged wider. In wriggled Aisyah.

Sarah hugged the woman, overjoyed to see her. "Where's Ruslan?" She needed to talk to him. Needed his advice on what to do now. "Ruslan?" she repeated.

Aisyah shrugged with spread hands to tell Sarah she didn't know.

He'd probably left for that village to find his father. Well, of course he would. He had every right to. He'd already gone out of his way to help her. Still, she wished he were here right now. Between the two of them they'd figure out something.

"Surf Cat's back," she said to Peter as she knelt back down beside him. "He brought Aisyah with him. Maybe the darn cat really is a genie."

Peter's eyes fluttered open, and he grinned at her and then at Aisyah. A feeble grin, but a grin. God, that made her feel good. She vowed to herself that if—*when* he got better, she would never ever tease him again. About anything. He could be as annoying as he wanted to. She wouldn't say a word. Well, maybe that was asking too much. But she'd be polite. She wouldn't yell *shut up*, she'd say *please be quiet*.

Aisyah had a small paper packet with her, which she ripped open and poured into the remaining water in the wash basin. The yellow powder made a paste, which she smeared on Peter's chest. The paste had a sharp, medicinal odor.

"*Jamu*," Aisyah said.

Traditional medicine. Better than nothing. Might even be better than aspirin.

But what Peter really needed was proper medicine and hospital care.

Dad, Dad, what am I supposed to do now?

Surf Cat licked his paws, offering no clues. But wait—he looked like he was praying. Sort of praying, anyhow. Was that a sign she was to pray? She didn't want to. What good was prayer? Just wishful thinking. When people were helpless and had no more options, that's when they prayed. A last resort for the desperate. That wasn't her. She'd get Peter help somehow.

Peter stroked Surf Cat's fur. Boy, his fingernails needed trimming. Cleaning. She looked down at hers. She hadn't thought about them once in days. Bitten down to nubs. An awful old habit, back again.

Aisyah rubbed the paste on Peter's face. "Hey," he said, trying to push her hand away.

"It's medicine," Sarah said. Her brother relaxed. When Aisyah was done, Peter caught Sarah's smile. "What?" he asked suspiciously.

"Remember how you always made fun of Mom's facials? You look just like that now. Wish I had a camera."

"Sheesh." He lifted a hand to rub off the drying paste. Sarah caught his hand, folded his fingers into her own. "It's medicine, honest."

"You won't tell anybody? You won't tell Ben and Charlie?" They were his two best friends.

"No, just Amanda."

"Not her! She's the world's biggest blabbermouth!"

"Just kidding. I won't tell a soul. Promise. Except Dad."

Peter scowled. "Okay. You can tell him. Nobody else, though." He closed his eyes and drowsed off again. The paste seemed to be helping, as his breathing seemed to come easier, his constant coughing and chuffing tapering off.

Still, worry was a rat loose in Sarah's stomach, gnawing away with its big, sharp teeth.

A distant wailing drifted on the dusk. Aisyah tugged at Sarah's arm, asking her to come. *Not for long*, she gestured. Peter seemed to be sleeping okay. Sarah squeezed out of the tent and hurried after Aisyah to the other hill.

A man stood at the front of a dusty clearing, facing the sunset as he chanted in that long wail. People gathered from the ramshackle huts, the men lining up in rows in front and the smaller group of women lining up in the back. The mute girl joined Aisyah in the last row. The girl caught Sarah's eye and gave her a smile, and then grew solemn as she raised her hands in prayer.

A sharp yearning seized Sarah. How wonderful it would be to have such faith.

She knelt down beside the girl. Prayer was to her a foreign language, and so her words were hesitant and awkward.

God, please help Peter get better. And help my dad and keep him safe. A hesitant pause. *And bless*

Mom in heaven. Weird to be praying for her dead mother and still not feel a thing. Next to her the girl stirred, and it was then that a fierce emotion rose in her. *And this girl, she has nobody, keep her safe too.*

Was God listening? She had no idea. He did not seem any closer or more real to her, but saying her prayer had calmed the gnawing rat in her stomach.

Chapter 23

The two men walked Ruslan over to the single tree, its shadow growing long across a dead rice field. A crow had settled on its branches, the bird black as a devil from hell. Ruslan's heart banged away, but whatever happened, he wasn't going to go with the rebels. He had to find his father.

"Clever, that little slip you gave us, falling into the river like that," the rebel leader with the white eye said. The other man stood respectfully to the side. "But I knew you could swim. Your father was always so proud of you. Told us how you were like a fish, playing in the sea."

Ruslan gaped at him.

"I'm Bachtiar. Your mother's half brother.

Your uncle." His good eye held Ruslan's gaze, as though waiting for Ruslan's reaction.

Ruslan couldn't speak. This man was his *uncle*? Things seemed to be getting very complicated very quickly here. He finally spluttered the only thing that came to mind. "How come you didn't tell me before?"

"I would have, if you hadn't been so hasty in leaving us. I would have also told you that your father never made it past Calang. The military intelligence intercepted him and took him in for questioning."

That drove all other thoughts from Ruslan's mind. "Do you know what happened to him?"

The man—his uncle—shook his head. "The interrogation unit worked out of a building by the officers' mess. Gone. Nobody would have made it out of those cells."

Ruslan bit the inside of his cheek, hard. "My father would have."

His uncle's good eye softened. "Let me tell you something. Your mother wasn't killed in a cross fire. She died as a fighter, a rifle in her hands. She was a proud Acehnese warrior, fighting for a free Aceh. After her death your father took you away from Ie Mameh, refusing to let you grow up in the cause. We respected that. But now he is dead. Killed by the military just as surely as if they'd shot him."

The silence that followed was broken by the loud flapping of the crow's wings. The bird soared on the golden air, gliding down to the second open grave pit. The operator had shut down the excavator for the day. He bent over a plastic bucket, rinsing his face.

Ruslan's uncle put a hand on his shoulder. "We're your family now, Ruslan. Come with us. Not as rebel, but as family." His uncle kissed Ruslan on both cheeks in a formal hug. His skin was rough, his breath smelled of tobacco, but his touch was gentle.

Ruslan was in a daze. This man was his uncle. And hadn't his mother come to him today, to comfort him? It was as though somebody had knocked down a high wall within him, allowing him to see a grand vista of green land and gentle water that he had never known was there.

The crow flapped down into the grave pit. The excavator man saw and shouted, waving his hands. The bird flew out with lazy beats of its wings.

"I have to find my father," Ruslan said. "I have to know."

His uncle's smile reached even to his dead white eye. "As a good son must. When you are ready to find me, go to that small hill where you stayed the other night. Some of my men will be there."

The guard yelled at Ruslan, "Hey, sun's setting. We have to get back to camp."

"God go with you," Ruslan's uncle said. He and the other man walked away.

In the bouncing truck the guard sat beside Ruslan and shared a single cigarette with the excavator operator. He offered the cigarette to Ruslan, who declined. "Who were those guys?" the guard asked.

"Family," Ruslan said.

"Good to know you have some left."

Ruslan parked the truck in the cleared parking lot at the foot of the command hill. The truck driver was there, slouched on the seat of one of the few motor scooters the soldiers were using. He rubbed the back of his head, glaring at Ruslan, but said nothing, knowing that Ruslan could accuse him of corpse robbing.

As the other men wearily made their way up the hill, Ruslan trotted into the ruins of the town. All the living were already gathering on the camp's hill for sunset prayers and for their rations. The only inhabitants in this neighborhood were ghosts stirring on the dusk breeze, and it seemed to Ruslan he could almost hear their bewildered and agonized whispers. He quickly found the drawing pad and box of crayons that he had placed on top of the overturned car. There was no black crayon in the box, so he chose the dark blue. Turning to the first blank page, which was water-stained but still clean enough, he rapidly began to sketch a face. A gust of wind ruffled the corner of the page, and over his shoulder, the whispering grew louder. *No, no, draw me, draw my face, let them know it's me, give me back my name.*

With a shiver Ruslan slapped shut the drawing pad and hurried to the hill, where a man sang the call to prayer, his bare voice thin and reedy, yet rich with life.

Chapter 24

When the prayers were finished, Aisyah grabbed Sarah's hand and tugged her to the rations line. More rice gruel, served into coconut shells out of a big blackened pot. Sarah had no appetite, so she offered hers to the girl. The girl accepted with a grave nod of her head, and Sarah watched her daintily slurp the gruel, taking her time, unlike most of the others, who gulped theirs.

Moonlight had replaced twilight when Sarah finally headed back to the clinic. Several campfires also added a flickering glow to her uneven path. A shower of sparks rose from one of them. She glanced up. Somebody had added a chunk of wood. The figure turned, and she recognized Ruslan's slender frame and his slightly hunched shoulders.

A starburst of happiness filled her heart. "Ruslan!" she called out and ran up to him.

"Hello, Sarah," he said. An anxiety was in his voice that hadn't been there before. A heavy anxiety.

Her happiness faded a little. "What's wrong?"

"My father," he said. "He didn't make it to the village. He was stopped here and . . . and . . ." His voice caught. He cleared it with a cough. "He was caught in the tsunami."

"Oh." That was all she could say? Look at those eyes of his, how much he was hurting. She gestured at the people in the camp. "They all survived. Your dad did too. You must believe he did."

"Yes," Ruslan said. "Never give up hope." He had a sketch pad in his hand, and he squatted to draw something by the light of the fire.

Sarah sat beside him. The starburst of happiness was gone. Her own anxiety came bubbling up. "I'm really worried about Peter. There isn't any medicine here. Aisyah gave him some of that *jamu* stuff but he really needs proper treatment and medicine."

The way that girl had stopped her fight to breathe. Just like that. Gone.

The rat was back in her stomach, gnawing with vicious bites.

"Maybe there's medicine in Meulaboh," Ruslan

said. "The hospital there was high. The flood didn't reach it."

Sarah's brain grew lighter, lifted off her spine. "Ruslan! How come you didn't tell me before?"

"I didn't know you wanted to know." He wasn't paying full attention to her, concentrating on his drawing, the face of a man.

"God, Ruslan, if you'd told me about the hospital in Meulaboh, I would have gone there and not here."

"You kept talking about the doctor in Calang. What do I know about this doctor? I thought you knew."

Meulaboh. Now she had to get to Meulaboh. She was gathering her courage to ask for Ruslan's help, when something about the picture he was drawing caught her attention. She'd seen this man before, with his broad forehead and lopsided chin and slightly crooked teeth that Ruslan displayed in a kind smile. When Ruslan drew in the pupils, the drawing came alive. The man smiled at Sarah, as though ready to say hello.

"I know him," she said.

"Good. I'm going to show this to people, maybe they've seen him."

"Where have I seen him? It's right there, but I can't remember."

"You can't remember?" Ruslan said. "He worked on your boat engine." And then, with a touch of exasperation, "My father."

"That's not where I remember him from. . . . Wait, wait, I know. I saw him when I was in that little sailboat. He was on one of those children's water park boats, you know, with a rear paddle wheel."

Ruslan looked at her as though she were crazy. "On a paddleboat? I don't think so."

"He was riding it to Meulaboh, pedaling hard." The implication finally registered. "This was *after* the tsunami. God, Ruslan, he's *alive*."

Ruslan absorbed that with a blank face. What surfaced, though, wasn't elation but suspicion. He had Sarah repeat everything in greater detail, listening skeptically, and as she did so, her conviction grew stronger. "It's him, Ruslan, it's him. He was going to Meulaboh to look for *you*."

Ruslan took a deep ragged breath, his skepticism flattened into a stunned look. "I think I saw him too. I was walking on the beach. A Mickey Mouse boat."

"Yes, yes! A Mickey Mouse boat, and he was holding a pole, like in Venice. Mickey Mouse, I mean."

"And he was going to Meulaboh," Ruslan said.

"Both of them were going to Meulaboh," Sarah said.

With tears filling his eyes, Ruslan threw up his hands and exclaimed joyfully in his language. Then he grabbed her hand and pulled her in for a fervent kiss on both cheeks. His lips were soft and warm. For a fleeting second Sarah imagined them on her own. Then, as they awkwardly straightened, their lips did brush together in an accidental touch.

Ruslan jerked back. Even in this flickering light, she could see a dusky color rising up his slender neck. Could he see the same on hers?

"We must go to Meulaboh," Ruslan said. "We must go tonight."

"How?"

"I have family. We will ask them for help."

A soldier jogged up the hill and spoke to Ruslan. Sarah caught the word "commandant."

Ruslan put an arm around Sarah and drew her close to whisper in her ear. "The parking lot at the bottom of the hill. The big truck. Meet me there when the moon is in the middle of the sky. If I am not there when the moon is half down again, you must walk to that hill where we were before. One of my family will be there. He will take you to Meulaboh."

The soldier barked, prodding Ruslan to his feet with his rifle barrel.

"Remember," Ruslan said over his shoulder to her.

Sarah hurried to the clinic tent. A kerosene lantern had been hung from one of the aluminum ceiling struts. Its yellow flame cast a dim glow. The nurse had transferred Peter to the dead girl's cot. Sarah forced herself to relax. Didn't mean anything. The cot wasn't cursed. At least Peter was sleeping. Sweat beaded his neck, dripped down his chest, marking trails in the dried paste. His forehead felt cooler to her touch, but his breathing seemed just as labored.

A new nurse who looked as tired as the old one made rounds with the aspirin pills. Sarah couldn't bring herself to wake Peter to take his half. She went outside and used the latrines, which were planks over holes in the ground, a square of plastic sheeting providing privacy. The stench was thick enough to float her off the ground.

By a tree a short distance away, three soldiers in their underwear took a bucket bath from a well.

"Miss, you want bath?" one called out to her as she exited.

God, did she ever, but not with all those guys watching.

The soldier who'd spoken came over with a sarong. "You take bath, no problem," he said. "No problem." He had a kind smile. But it was the little boy in his eyes, the fear and the loneliness, that made Sarah return the smile and take the sarong. He gave her a sliver of soap and shooed away the other guys. Tucking the sarong around her shoulders, using that garment for her modesty, she bucketed water over herself. Salty as the other well where she'd had a rinse, but just as clean. As she bathed, she stomped on her dirty bikini bottom and her shorts and T-shirt. The soap left a wonderful fragrance on her skin. It felt almost sacrilegious to put her wet and still dirty clothes back on. She returned the wet sarong to the soldier and thanked him.

"No problem," he said again.

In the tent, she lay down by Peter's cot. She didn't want to sleep. Had to watch the moon. Middle of the sky, Ruslan had said. But sleep overtook her anyway. She woke in a panic, certain she'd overslept. But the moonlight on the tent's thin fabric was still low. Peter stirred and muttered in his dreams. Of what? Their mother, dancing?

She dozed and woke several times. Finally it was time. She shook Peter awake. "Peter, you have to go to the bathroom."

"Huh?"

"Come, I'll take you to the bathroom."

He was too disoriented to protest. She held his head, leading him out of the tent. The guard sleeping at the front desk groggily lifted his head from his cradling arms. "Bathroom," Sarah whispered to him. He put his head down again.

Outside the tent, Sarah picked Peter up and carried him with his arms slung around her neck. His ragged breaths were hot on her chin. She carried him along the darkest shadows of the hill's sparse tree line. In the moonlight the ruins of the town below her looked like chewed bones.

In the green command tent a bright light shone behind the canvas. Voices murmured. One rose in anger. A thud. Mocking laughter.

She hurried on. No one was about. The parking lot where the big truck stood had once been a school yard. Remnants of the playground's painted white lines were still visible. She scurried down a path bulldozed through the school's rubble to the parking lot, nearly tripping once on loose brick.

"Ruslan!" she whispered. "Ruslan!"

No reply. In the distance came the sound of waves surging on an unseen beach. Once that had been a soothing sound, but for a second her skin prickled, and she wanted to dash back up the hill.

She put Peter down in the deepest shadows, between the truck's rear wheels and a motor scooter. He came awake. "What are we doing?"

"Having more fun," she said.

"Are they looking for Dad yet?"

"He's looking for us." Sarah was certain of it. Her father was the sort of man who'd dig barehanded through a granite mountain to find his kids.

"Good. Where's Surf Cat?"

God. Where was that cat? "Chasing owls."

Peter smiled and closed his eyes with another bout of coughing.

No Ruslan. What had happened to him? Was he okay?

In the distance to the north, she thought she could make out the small hill against the silhouette of the bigger foothills. She tried not to worry about Ruslan. More worry wouldn't help. She stared up at the clear sky and made up her own silly constellations.

Then she slept for a while.

When the moon was halfway to the western horizon, she gathered Peter up in her arms and started walking down the cleared road toward the distant hill.

Chapter 25

With the tip of his finger, the commandant pushed a small photo across the plywood desk toward Ruslan. A pressure lantern hung from a hook above the desk, hissing out a hot white light. The stained photo was a mug shot of a man with one dead white eye.

"Don't know him," Ruslan said.

"Your mother's half brother. Your uncle. A rebel."

"I don't know any rebels."

The commandant leaned back and twirled an unlit cigarette in his fingers. "What good Acehnese boy doesn't know his own family?" he asked with mocking incredulity.

Ruslan looked up at him. Something swished its tail in his heart. *Keep your head*, he told himself. *Father is okay, he is in Meulaboh, that's the important thing.*

The commandant laughed. "Oh, you're giving me that look. I know that look. I've seen it in lots of rebel eyes. When I'm done with them, they don't have it anymore."

Another, larger swish, but what emerged in Ruslan's heart was not anger, but scorn tinged with pity. Ruslan put a finger on the photo and pushed it over to the commandant's side of the table. "This is the world before. Now the world is different. This doesn't matter anymore."

The commandant stuck the cigarette in his mouth and rose to his feet to press the tip against the hot lantern glass. The tip smoldered and then glowed. He inhaled deeply and sat back down in a billow of smoke. He stared flatly at Ruslan. Ruslan held his gaze.

"You're just a boy," the commandant said. "Who are you to be telling me what matters?"

Ruslan didn't reply.

The commandant exhaled another cloud of smoke and then lunged across the table, smashing Ruslan on the cheek with his clenched fist. The blow sent Ruslan sprawling to the floor, where he lay stunned. He heard, as if from a great distance, the commandant laughing and telling one of his men to take Ruslan away and guard him until morning. The soldier put an arm under his shoulders and yanked him to his feet.

The soldier tied his hands with rope and led him into the night to tether him to a tree, as if he were a goat. "Sorry," the soldier muttered, and left him there. When the pain of his cheek subsided, Ruslan worked at the rope around his hands, but the knots were too tight. He sat down in the dirt and watched the moon rise into the sky. Sarah would be at the truck by now, waiting for him. He hoped she remembered what he'd told her, to start for the hill when he didn't show. She had to get Peter proper help as soon as she could. Ruslan was an artist, and an artist bravely sees the truth of things. What Ruslan could see was death's long arm stealing closer to the boy.

The soldier slipped out of the trees and knelt by him. "You are right," he whispered to Ruslan. "Some things don't matter anymore." He cut Ruslan's binds with a knife. "Go now, and quickly. The commandant doesn't sleep well. He might call you back any moment. God be with you, with us all." The soldier stole back into the trees.

Ruslan ran in a half crouch down the hill, flexing

his painful hands. Sarah wasn't in the parking lot. Good. She'd have started on her way.

He cracked open the driver's door and edged inside. The keys weren't in the ignition, and they weren't in the glove box. He was annoyed at this—who would want to steal a lousy dump truck? Where could anybody take it, anyway? But no matter. He knew how to hot-wire, one of the benefits of having a mechanic for a father. He felt underneath the dashboard and pulled out the ignition wires. It was impossible to tell the colors in this light. He picked two and stripped them with his teeth.

From up the hill came the commandant's harsh and penetrating voice. "Go find him, now. Don't come back without him."

The wires didn't work. He picked another one. Through the windshield he could see a dozen men starting to search the hill, working their way down.

Finally, on his third try, the engine turned over. He jammed the gears into reverse and backed out of the lot faster than a devil out of a mosque. On the hill, soldiers shouted and began running. He shoved the gear into first. A shadow jumped through the open passenger window, and in his alarm Ruslan nearly banged his head on the cab's roof. But it was only Peter's spooky orange cat. "Can you make us vanish from sight?" he muttered. A gun fired, the bullet clanging into the metal bed of the truck. Ruslan stepped on the accelerator, thrusting through the gears. "Come on, come on, come on," he urged. The truck leisurely picked up speed, tires kicking up a cloud of moonlit dust.

He had no idea where Sarah and Peter were, but surely they were using the road, which was the only cleared path toward the hill. After a minute he switched on the headlights, the better to spot them. He caught a flash of something ducking behind a mound of dirt and braked hard to a stop, the cloud of dust filling up the cab. He called out, "Sarah, Sarah, it's me, quick, get in, get in."

She emerged from the side of the road, Peter in her arms, and ran to the truck, coughing at the dust. Ruslan flung open the passenger-side door and grabbed Peter from her. Sarah hadn't even closed the door when he stomped on the accelerator.

"Hey, it's Surf Cat," Peter said. "Catch any owls?"

In the side view mirrors, Ruslan could see through the dust the headlights of motor scooters slowly growing brighter as they gave chase. He cursed himself for not having spiked their tires. A burst of gunfire chattered over the engine's roar. He pushed Peter's head down onto Sarah's lap.

The graveyard flashed by, the excavator looking like a sleeping beast. The truck came to the end of the cleared road and barreled over clumps of swamp grass that the tsunami had scattered on the asphalt. The road dipped into a greasy swamp, oily swirls reflecting in the truck's headlights. Ruslan shoved the brake pedal to the floor. The truck shuddered and squealed to a stop. A hundred yards beyond, Ruslan could see the road rise up again out of the swamp and continue on. He had no idea how deep the swamp was.

Over the idling engine, he could hear the whine of the motor scooters growing louder. In the side view mirrors the beam of their headlights grew brighter and brighter.

Chapter 26

Sarah stared at the bright lights in the rearview mirror and then looked at Ruslan. He appeared calm, as though he had all the time in the world to make a decision. His cheek, she noticed, was bruised. He revved the engine and popped the clutch. The truck shot forward and accelerated into the mud. Over the engine and splattering of mud, she could hear gunshots. The passenger side view mirror shattered, shards of glass peppering her in the face.

The truck started sliding and slipping. "*Ayo, ayo, ayo,*" Ruslan chanted. She joined in, changing the words of an old childhood story. "I know you can, I know you can, I know you can."

But maybe the truck couldn't. It slowed and

sank deeper. God, how deep was the swamp? What if it swallowed them up? Should she get Peter onto the roof of the cab? The wheels gripped hard again, and the truck lumbered out of the mud. Several more gunshots rang out. A hole appeared neat as a magic trick in the windshield. Ruslan grabbed Sarah's head and shoved her to the seat over Peter.

She jerked upright and gave him a glare. "Don't do that again."

"Not safe."

"You don't have to shove me, just tell me."

She could see his bruised cheek tighten. "Will you get down, please?"

Then she realized how dumb she was. People were *shooting* at them. She bent tight over Peter, who in turn held Surf Cat in his arms.

The truck swayed and lurched as Ruslan steered around obstacles and sometimes over them. Several minutes later he said, "We're okay now. We can't go anymore. We'll have to walk the rest of the way."

She sat up. Downed oil palm trees blocked the road ahead, with no way around for the truck. In the distance a small fire burned on top of the hillock they had camped on. Ruslan pulled some wires, and the engine quit with one final shudder.

The night's cool silence filled the cab. The only noise was Peter's raspy breathing.

"Sorry I snapped at you," Sarah said. "I wasn't thinking. My dad sometimes says that if anyone tapped me on the head, my brain would pop out my—" She caught herself, could feel herself coloring.

"Your *pantat*," Ruslan said.

Sarah chuckled. "Is that how you say it?"

Ruslan grinned and then winced, pressing his fingers to his cheek.

She reached up and took his hand away, and touched her own fingers to the bruise. "Does that hurt bad?"

"Not so bad."

On the seat between them Peter coughed and said, "You guys gonna yak all night? I don't feel so good. I wanna sleep."

They got out of the cab and started to hike. Sarah and Ruslan took turns carrying him, although Ruslan carried him the longest and farthest. Sarah was grateful for that.

The eastern sky was already graying with light when they came to the hillock. Two young men had spotted them and were waiting. They spoke briefly with Ruslan in the local language and shyly but curiously shook hands with Sarah.

"Your family?" Sarah asked Ruslan.

"Not yet."

One of the men took Peter, swinging him onto his back for a piggyback ride. They started to walk again. The gray light strengthened. By the time the top of the sun had cracked the horizon, they'd come to the first of the green rice fields. Here was life as it had been, before the world had tilted. A Jeep was parked on a badly potholed but otherwise ordinary road, clear of any flood debris. From a stand of trees by the road appeared another group of three men, armed with rifles. The man who led them had an eye that was an ugly swirl of white.

"My uncle," Ruslan murmured to Sarah.

With his good eye, Ruslan's uncle gave Sarah an assessing look that was neither unfriendly nor welcoming, and then hugged Ruslan. Ruslan, Sarah noticed, did not return the embrace.

His uncle pointed to the bruise on his cheek. Ruslan gestured impatiently at that, and then spoke softly and swiftly. *Bapa*, Sarah heard him say, *Meulaboh*. He nodded at Sarah. His hands mimed what his words were saying, his father pedaling a water park boat.

The uncle's good eye widened in astonishment. He turned to Sarah. "Yes?" he said in English.

"Yes," Sarah said. She felt jittery with impatience. She needed to get Peter to the Meulaboh hospital.

The man lifted his chin and roared with laughter.

"He thinks it's funny, my father on a child's toy," Ruslan muttered to Sarah. But when the man's amusement died, he lifted his hands and said a prayer that was clearly one of thanksgiving.

Ruslan nodded at Peter, still on the young man's back, and said a few urgent words. The uncle listened, a frown of concern gathering on his face. He felt Peter's neck and then barked an order at the young man, who put Peter down in the backseat of the Jeep.

Ruslan turned to Sarah. "He'll take us as far as he can."

Sarah wanted to fly to Meulaboh's hospital. Wanted to be there *now*.

They all jammed into the boxy little car, Sarah rigid between Ruslan and the door, with Peter stretched out on their laps and Surf Cat on the floor mat between her feet. Ruslan leaned forward and gave his uncle a gold ring, saying something about it. The uncle read the inscription in the band, and then nodded and put it in his shirt pocket. What was all that about? But Sarah was too tired to ask. She closed her eyes and fell asleep. When she woke, she found her head was on Ruslan's shoulder. She straightened and drowsily watched a village of houses on stilts flash past. A mosque, crowded with people.

"Refugees," Ruslan said.

Sarah closed her eyes again, determined to remain upright. But Ruslan's shoulder was irresistible. She gave up and leaned against him, snuggling to find the most comfortable position. When she woke next, his head was leaning against hers, his breathing a light snore.

She extricated herself and adjusted Peter's weight on her lap. Her heart jolted when she noticed that the tips of his fingers were getting a bluish tinge. God, couldn't they go any faster?

The Jeep turned down into the ruined coast, the driver making his way through a road that a handful of men were clearing. He stopped by the edge of a river, a remnant of a bridge still spanning it. They all got out, the driver taking Peter off Sarah's lap. Ruslan's uncle said something to Ruslan, pointing to tin roofs glinting in a valley on the other side of the river. With a stick he drew a map in the dirt, which Ruslan studied.

"Relief aid helicopters are beginning to make food drops at this village," Ruslan said to Sarah. "We go and wait for one."

"How do we cross the river?"

"That." Ruslan nodded at the narrow metal span.

Sarah moaned. "I can't. I'm afraid of heights."

"I did it before. It's easy. Don't worry."

Using a big duffel bag from the back of the Jeep, the men fashioned a secure sling for Peter. The two young men would take him across.

Ruslan's uncle shook hands with Sarah, saying, "Good luck" in English. He hugged Ruslan again. This time Ruslan returned the hug with a smile that slowly became bemusement as he and Sarah walked down to the bridge's embankment. "I have family now," he said with wonder.

Sarah scarcely heard him. That tiny little span fifty feet above the water consumed her attention. The men carrying Peter stepped confidently onto the metal I-beam, Surf Cat trotting behind them. They were already halfway across when Ruslan finally badgered Sarah into taking her first step onto the girder, right behind him. She gripped a guy wire with one hand, her other hand holding on to Ruslan's. She took a second step. A third. Now she had to let go of the guy wire and take several steps to the second wire.

All the space around her and the long drop below to the muddy water made her freeze up. She clung to the guy wire, moaning. "I can't, I can't, I can't."

"You have to," Ruslan said, his tone now frustrated and angry with her.

She squeezed her eyes shut. *Please, Dad, help me.*

Her father was silent.

"Peter is waiting," Ruslan said, in a softer voice. "Think of Peter."

Peter. Peter needed her. She had to cross this bridge for her brother.

And so she did, one nervous step at a time, not daring to hold on to a guy wire for too long in case she couldn't let go again. When she at last jumped off onto solid ground on the other side, Ruslan said, "Now, that was easy, wasn't it?"

She looked back and shivered. "No, it wasn't. I don't want to ever do that again."

A man rode into view on a yellow trail bike and swung off to give it to Ruslan. Ruslan laughed in what sounded like disbelief. "Our new ride," he said.

"We're going on that?"

"It's okay. I've driven this before. I'm an expert at this trail bike."

Ruslan tucked Surf Cat between his legs. Sarah swung onto the saddle seat behind him. The two young men helped sandwich Peter between Ruslan and Sarah.

"Drive fast," she told Ruslan.

He drove fast. At first she gingerly clasped his

waist, but after one sharp turn, she decided it was safer for her and Peter to wrap her arms around him. She leaned her head against his back. It felt safe, secure.

Soon they came to a small village, its mosque crowded with refugees. Across the road from the mosque was a weedy soccer field, a big white *H* painted on the centerline. "That must be the helicopter landing," Ruslan said over his shoulder. "We'll wait at the mosque."

He parked the trail bike outside the mosque's gate and lowered Surf Cat to the ground. Sarah carried Peter to the shade of the wide verandah. Squatting on the tiled steps were a dozen or so dirty and ragged men with the blackened skin of fishermen, their unblinking eyes staring at nothing. Sarah sat to their side, with Peter's head resting on her lap. His breaths came shorter and harder, and his fingertips were a touch bluer.

"When will the helicopter come?" she asked Ruslan.

"I'll ask." Ruslan approached one of the villagers helping at the mosque and returned with the answer. "Soon," he said.

Soon could be forever. Sarah stroked Peter's head as she searched the sky, fiercely willing the helicopter to appear.

One of the young fishermen stirred and rose from his haunches. A fire burned beneath his skeletal face. He asked Sarah a question in a tentative voice, as though he had to search for words.

Ruslan said, "He says can you help him." The man continued speaking, words coming faster to him now.

Ruslan translated. "His whole village is all gone from the tsunami, more than two hundred people. Only sixteen men alive. Women and children and elders gone. They saw the wave, but only the young men could run fast enough. This man tried to help his wife and baby, but they were too slow and he had to leave them behind to save his own life." Ruslan blinked rapidly and his voice trembled, but he finished the translation. "He hasn't slept since. He asks can you help him sleep."

The man was looking at Sarah, but his gaze was so haunted that she wondered if he were really seeing her. She lifted her hand from her brother's head to reach out and touch him. "I'm so sorry, I wish I had something."

His smile was nothing, just a reflex, and he retreated to his silent, sleepless world. Sarah resumed her anxious scrutiny of the sky. A minute later she heard the faint *whop-whop-whop* of several helicopters before she saw them, three dots against the clouds. Two helicopters raced overhead, but one curved in a sharp descent to the soccer field. Village children pranced with excitement on the sideline.

"Let's go," she said. Ruslan took Peter in his arms, and they hurried out to the field. The helicopter was a military one, with a painted flag on its side that Sarah didn't recognize. It settled delicately onto the grass with a great billowing wind. The roaring blades slowed but kept spinning as two helmeted men in green uniforms jumped out and began to manhandle boxes of noodles and bags of rice out of the chopper's belly.

Sarah ran out to them, Ruslan right behind her, cradling Peter. One of the men, a handsome Indian, looked at her with mild surprise. She leaned close to his head and shouted as loudly as she could, "Can you give us a ride to Meulaboh?"

The man spoke into his helmet microphone. The pilot looked through his cockpit window and waved them aboard. The crewman strapped the three of them into a row of aluminum and vinyl seats in the back of the helicopter and gave them earmuffs to wear against the noise.

The chopper took off. The door had been removed, and through the open space, Sarah saw the upturned faces of waving children dwindling to blobs. Rice paddies became patterns of geometry. Then, without warning, the green land turned brown and shattered, trees and bushes all flattened in one direction, away from the coast. Sarah craned her head and saw the shore in the distance.

Ruslan wasn't watching. He'd spotted a notebook and pen in a side pouch and was sketching his father's face again.

Then she remembered: Surf Cat. They'd left Surf Cat behind.

Peter leaned against her, his eyes half-lidded, his chest heaving with the effort of his breathing, and she forgot all about Surf Cat. "Hurry, hurry, hurry," she shouted at the pilot, but of course he couldn't hear her.

The helicopter swung over a warren of undamaged houses and descended to a big field surrounded on three sides by military looking barracks. People bustled about, soldiers of various countries in various uniforms as well as other Westerners and Asians. A red-haired woman in a skirt and blouse held a microphone to one of the Western military men in tan fatigues. Filming them with a shoulder video camera was a man with a scruffy goatee. None of it made any sense to Sarah. It all seemed so utterly surreal.

The chopper's skids settled on the ground.

Sarah yanked off her and Peter's earmuffs and seat belts and bolted out of the helicopter with Peter in her arms even before the crewmen were out of their seats. Ruslan was right behind her.

"Where's the hospital?" she shouted at Ruslan over the dying roar of the engine.

"This is military headquarters," he shouted back. "We need a car, too far to walk. We can try to find one on the main road."

Still carrying Peter, Sarah ran to the side of the field. The red-haired woman looked at her and then abruptly lowered the microphone from the soldier's mouth. She rushed over to Sarah, her skirt snapping against her legs. The cameraman scuttled after her.

"You aren't Sarah Bedford, are you?" the woman asked. "And your brother Peter?"

"I need to get him to a hospital quick," Sarah said.

The woman took in Sarah's ragged appearance, the way she held Peter. "You look perfect," the woman said. "And keep holding your brother like that. Just perfect." She stood by Sarah's side, clutching her arm behind the elbow, as though to keep her from fleeing. The cameraman aimed his lens at them. The woman said brightly, "I am here at Meulaboh, West Aceh, with an exclusive interview with the missing Bedford children, whom I've just found. Sarah, the whole world has been wondering what has happened to you and your brother. Would you like to fill us in?"

"He's sick," Sarah said. "I need to get him to a hospital. Do you have a car?"

"Tell us the events of December twenty-sixth, when you and your family were caught by the tsunami. You were on your yacht, sailing to Malaysia, is that correct?"

By this time many of the busy people rushing back and forth around the barracks had paused to watch them. A man peeked out of the louvered windows of the nearest building and a moment later darted around the corner, the sharp creases of his khaki safari suit slicing the air, with his cameraman on his heels.

The woman lowered her microphone to snap, "George, this is my exclusive."

The man ignored her and stood on Sarah's other side, in front of Ruslan. Facing his cameraman, he said, "In another amazing development, we have managed to locate Sarah and Peter Bedford."

"Piss off, George," the woman said. "I was the one who found them first."

He shoved his microphone into Sarah's face. "Sarah, what's your story? Where were you and your family when the tsunami hit?"

"I need a ride to the hospital," Sarah pleaded. "Please, a car, does anybody have a car?"

More journalists and cameramen came running across the soccer field, one guy staggering along with a satellite dish. They surrounded Sarah and Peter, pushing and shoving for the best positions. The red-headed woman wielded her elbow like a weapon, but to little effect. A swarm of microphones circled Sarah's head. A dozen simultaneous questions in various English accents peppered the air, a bombardment of voices that confused and frightened her.

Peter's arms slid off her neck. She struggled to hold his weight as he sucked air with jerky gasps. His lips were blue. "For God's sake, everybody," Sarah shouted, "I need to get my brother to a hospital!"

The woman thrust her microphone at Peter to capture his tortured breaths. Her cameraman moved in for a close-up of Peter's face, his eyes fluttering. Other cameras jostled for position.

"Somebody help me!" Sarah screamed.

The tall Western soldier whom the woman had been interviewing pushed through the crowd, his cap bobbing above the others' heads. In her fright and confusion, Sarah thought he was going to add to the chaos, but then she noticed the black-lettered tags on his khaki tunic. His name was Hertzig, and he was a U.S. Marine. She had no idea why a U.S.

Marine would be here, yet here he was, big as life.

"Help me," she begged. "My brother swallowed a lot of dirty water."

He took one sharp look at Peter and bellowed at someone across the soccer field. "Crosley, get the corpsmen over here with the oxygen! On the double!" Taking Peter from her arms, he bulled his way through the journalists. Other marines ran across the field, carrying a stretcher and medical kits. They transferred Peter to the stretcher. One corpsman slapped an oxygen mask onto his face as they rushed him into the shade of a tree. They knelt around him and treated him with swift but calm movements, putting a tube down his mouth, sticking needles into his arm. Sarah held her brother's limp hand. His blue fingertips flushed to red, the color of a miracle, and she felt like weeping with relief.

The marine named Hertzig, clearly an officer of some kind, ordered another marine with a radio pack to call the ship for an urgent medevac for the Bedford children and to pass the word on to the captain.

The journalists circled the stretcher. The woman journalist knelt beside Sarah and murmured in her ear, "We'll give you ten thousand dollars for an exclusive interview."

George said in her other ear, "We'll double whatever she offered."

She could have punched both of them. She shouted, "Will you please leave us alone!"

Officer Hertzig spread his long arms and said, "You heard her, everyone. Back off, back off now."

Another military helicopter shot onto the soccer field. "That's us," Officer Hertzig said to Sarah. "We'll take you and your brother out to the ship. He'll get as good medical care there as anywhere."

"Do you know where my dad is?"

Officer Hertzig shook his head. "There's been no word on him."

"We were on Tiger Island. My mom's dead. He had a broken leg. We need to look for him."

Officer Hertzig nodded calmly. "We can best organize the search from the ship."

The corpsmen carried Peter to the helicopter, where a doctor was waiting. Sarah searched the crowd and spotted Ruslan to the side, watching her, the notebook curled in his hand. She ran over to him. She wanted to give him a hug, but everyone was looking on, with many of the journalists still aiming their cameras at her. "Thanks so much, Ruslan," she said, trying to put into her voice more than just what the words themselves could carry.

He gave her a small smile that slid into her heart like a drug.

One of the helicopter's crewmen tugged at her elbow. "I'll be back to meet your father," she said, and gave him a final wave before boarding.

As the helicopter lifted from the ground, Sarah peered out the window. She spotted Ruslan on the road below, showing the sketch in the notebook to the driver of a truck draped with a huge International Red Cross banner.

She sat back, the lingering warmth of Ruslan's smile and the tremendous relief of having Peter safe giving way to a new urgency. She had her own dad to find.

Chapter 27

Despite the International Red Cross banners draped on the truck's sides, Ruslan recognized the big green Fuso diesel as one his father had worked on. The driver, with the trucker's standard aura of cigarette smoke and road grime, lounged on the front seat, suspiciously examining an unwrapped stick of chewing gum. His frown turned to a smile in cordial response to Ruslan's interruption.

"Haven't seen him," he said after studying Ruslan's sketch. "Not too many Ujung Karang residents survived, you know."

"My father did."

"They all say that," the driver said. "People running around showing pictures of their kids, their parents, their family. Nobody wants to accept the reality that they're dead and probably won't be found." He grimaced in apology. "Sorry, kid, I shouldn't be so blunt."

An image of the Calang dump truck rose like a specter. Ruslan forced it away. "No, he really did survive. A friend saw him after the tsunami."

He glanced up at the sky as he said that, but the helicopter was no longer in sight. Sarah had said she'd be back, but he wondered how, wondered when, even wondered why. He'd only known her for a few days, but even so, he felt a bewildering ache, of something wonderful gone before it was even glimpsed.

"You're one of the very few lucky ones, then," the driver said. He held up the stick of gum. "An American soldier gave this to me. You think it's poisoned with pig fat?"

Ruslan had been astounded to see the U.S. military on Acehnese soil, but that astonishment had quickly faded when he also noticed soldiers from France and Australia and Singapore, and civilians from a dozen Western and Asian countries. One of the French soldiers had offered him a curious elongated loaf of bread, which he had devoured in seconds.

"Poisoned with pig fat?" he said. "Why on earth would you think that?"

The driver shrugged. "That's what some people are saying. Westerners trying to corrupt us."

"That's stupid. If you don't want it, you can give it to me."

The driver winked and stuffed the gum into his mouth. "Hey, kid, good luck with your father. Really. God knows we need all the happiness we can get."

Ruslan walked down the bumpy street, which looked as it always had, dusty weeds along the sides, wires tangled up in tree branches, chickens scratching in the front yards. But the evidence of the tsunami was everywhere. In one front yard a family rinsed tin sheets and buckets of nails salvaged from their downtown hardware shop. On other porches sat listless people who had no jobs to go to, many sharing what little they had with homeless relatives who had nothing left. They listened kindly to Ruslan but regarded his sketch with drained eyes and shook their heads.

At the corner, where the street intersected the main road to Bergang, several canvas tents had been erected on the grounds of a small neighbo hood mosque. Refugees crowded its patio, catching whatever cool breeze they could. A hand-lettered cardboard sign, the ink still wet, had been placed on the waist-high fence, announcing in both

Indonesian and English that Muslim attire was mandatory for all those entering the property. Two Western men, wearing the T-shirts of an emergency civil engineer corps, their plump pink legs extending out of khaki shorts, were taking photos of the sign.

"Bunch of narrow-minded fundamentalist jihadists," one man said to his companion. "Chop off your head if you step foot inside."

Sharply angered, Ruslan said to him, "They ask only for common courtesy. And you do not have trousers to wear in public?"

The man whistled. "Hey, you speak good English. Want to earn some money as our interpreter? You look like you could use a pair of pants yourself."

Ruslan ignored him and opened the gate. The refugees were from another district of town, and although many knew Ruslan's father, they hadn't seen him. They suggested he try the refugees camped out on the enormous front lawn of the mayor's splendid building.

The half-mile trudge to the mayor's office under the searing sun made him thirsty, and as he lined up for drinking water at an emergency tank, he showed his sketch. A woman told him that some Ujung Karang refugees were sheltering at the Grand Mosque, and after he'd slaked his thirst, he continued his march.

The Grand Mosque had been untouched by quake and water. He showed his sketch along the rows of tents. At the last row, beside the mosque's gleaming portico, a woman bent over a wood fire cooking relief-aid noodles. "He looks familiar," she said. "Was he here? I'm not sure. You can ask the Imam." She nodded over Ruslan's shoulder.

Ruslan turned his head. There in the shade of the portico stood the bearded cleric who had denounced Ruslan's art as ungodly. His hooded gaze took in the notebook, and he summoned Ruslan with a curl of his fingers.

With a sour exhalation Ruslan obeyed and handed him the pad. The cleric might tear up the sketch, but he'd draw a dozen, a hundred.

"My father," Ruslan said defiantly. "Have you seen him?"

The cleric stroked his beard as he studied the drawing. "Yusuf the mechanic. Excellent likeness." His eyes twinkled, and his mustache stretched out with his broad smile. "He was here this morning looking for you."

Ruslan's heart leaped. "Where is he now?"

"I saw him get on an ambulance carrying corpses to Bergang, where they are being buried." The cleric handed back the pad. "I have a motorcycle with some fuel. You may borrow it."

After profuse thanks, Ruslan drove off sedately, as befitting an unlicensed boy borrowing a cleric's well-kept motorcycle, but once around the corner, he threw open the throttle and bent over the handle-bars.

He didn't have to ask directions for the mass burial ground at Bergang. He caught up to a truck turning off onto the unpaved road leading past the Raiders' hill camp, where he had been detained and from which he had escaped days before. Six men wearing boots, gloves, and face masks stood in the back of the truck's bed, loaded with several dozen dark green plastic bags. Despite the plastic, the stench was overpowering, and Ruslan slowed down.

A soldier sat at the guard post, holding a hand-kerchief to his face. He was not in the least interested in Ruslan, who followed the truck past a sawmill. Beyond the mill, the truck stopped by the side of a small stream, where a fifty-foot-square pit had been dug in the ground, the gouge of orange earth raw as a wound. The truck backed up to the pit, beeping loudly. A dozen men stood around the pit, all wear-ing gloves and masks, including the cleric, ready to lay a symbolic white cloth on the plastic body bags and to say the prayer for the dead. Two men stood by with tanks of disinfectant strapped onto their backs and spray hoses in their hands.

Ruslan parked the motorcycle beside several others. He didn't see his father. As the men on the truck began to sling the body bags into the deep hole, he climbed the stream embankment. Within the mass grave three people stood on its steep sides, two women and a man, white masks over their faces. They reached out and unzipped the tossed body bags, looking at the bloated corpses within. The women examined only the children, but the man, his back to Ruslan, carefully studied the larger corpses. With the last one checked, he climbed up to the top of the pit and pressed the back of his visibly trembling hand against his forehead, pressing hard, as though he wished to crush his skull, his fingernails clenched deep into his palm.

At that gesture, each cell of Ruslan's skin prickled. He felt as though he were floating off the ground. He opened his mouth to call out for his father but could make no sound.

His father's fingers sprang open. He lowered his hand and turned to meet Ruslan's gaze. For several seconds he stood still.

And then he ran to meet his son.

Chapter 28

The plain gold band in Sarah's palm glinted in the bright lights of the ship's morgue. Her mother's wedding ring, given to her by the chaplain. The search team, still scouring Tiger Island's jungle and the surrounding sea for her father, had recovered her mother's remains. She was now behind cold steel doors.

The chaplain hovered by Sarah's shoulder. Probably anticipating a flood of grief. The doctor on her other side no doubt had a tranquilizer at the ready.

She studied the ring. Felt nothing. She wished the doctor had a medicine to help her feel something. What was wrong with her? When she at last turned away, her eyes dry as stone, the chaplain gave her a curious look but remained silent.

Peter was in the sick bay's intensive care. Recovering well, the doctors said. He was, too. During her last visit to see him, Peter had asked about Surf Cat. Off chasing mice, Sarah said.

It was great being back with people who understood her. Yet there was a sense in which they didn't understand at all, not the way Ruslan did.

Had he found his father yet? She was sure he had. She tried to envision their joyous reunion, but the scene kept slipping away from her.

The ship's media officer appeared in the doorway. "It's time to get ready," he said to Sarah.

There'd been such intense international media interest in the Bedford Children's Tsunami Drama (as headlined in one major newspaper) that it was decided—by whom, Sarah wasn't sure—to have a single press conference. Sarah would read a prepared account of her story, which the ship's media officer had helped her write. The press conference was going to be held on Meulaboh's military base, which also served as international relief headquarters.

The ship's captain had earlier ordered clothes for her and Peter from a big shopping mall in Medan, the closest city. Jeans and tops, and, as she had embarrassedly whispered to one of his aides, underwear as well. For the press conference, though, she wanted to wear a long-sleeved dress, or at least a skirt and blouse.

"No problem," the ship's media officer said, "if you don't mind wearing secondhand."

In a nook of the enormous ship were several crates of donated clothes that had not yet made it to shore. Sarah found a decorous long-sleeved dress in a blue flower print with an embroidered white collar. Not at all her style, but it fit.

"I'd like a scarf to cover my head," she said.

"I don't think there are any here," the officer said. "These are all clothes, not accessories."

"Can we get one somewhere?"

"You're not going to a mosque, just a press conference."

"It's still their country. I'd like to wear one. A sign of respect."

The media officer grumpily replied that he'd see what he could do.

Sarah arrived in the late afternoon at the military compound, wearing a plain blue scarf borrowed from one of the ship's female crew. The media officer escorted her. When she descended from the helicopter and saw the array of satellite dishes outside the building she was to speak in, and the crowd of people within, her nerves nearly failed her. She'd always hated speaking in public. Now she was going to stand in front of the whole world.

Officials were standing by to receive her. An orange cat drowsed in the arms of one Indonesian officer, who stepped forward to Sarah with a smile. "Yours, I think?" he said.

"Surf Cat!" Sarah exclaimed with delight, taking the cat from the man's arms to kiss its furry head. She turned to Officer Hertzig, whom she now knew to be a major. "This is Peter's cat. He'll be real happy to see him. Is it possible for Surf Cat to get a ride out to the boat?"

Major Hertzig winked. "The ship. Yeah, I think it's possible. I'll take care of it. Come here, kitty."

The media officer murmured in her ear, "Sarah, people are waiting."

She gathered up her nerves and shook hands with the local military commander and several other dignitaries. A plump man in a blue UN vest and a bandaged elbow gave her a reproachful look, murmuring, "You really should have come with us." She recognized him as one of the two men from the red helicopter.

The military commander ushered her into the building. At the front was a long table covered in green baize. In the center of the table, in front of a metal folding chair, sprouted a miniature forest of microphones. The commander pulled out the chair for Sarah. The intense heat was as smothering as a blanket, but thankfully, the media officer aimed one of the floor fans on her. She was acutely aware of the battery of cameras trained on her, and the pack of journalists behind them, holding recorders and note-books at the ready.

She read her speech. This was her story, but it felt as though she were reading about another girl.

As she read, she sensed something was not right. Aisyah. The mute girl. The story said nothing about them. To not mention them seemed wrong. She put down the sheets of paper. Looking directly at the cameras, she spoke of them, and of Ruslan, too, and the telling at last became her own story.

Yet a funny thing—the journalists didn't seem to care about that. They wanted more of her. Just her and Peter. The media officer filtered their shouted questions, allowing Sarah to reply to indi-vidual ones.

Yes, her brother was doing fine, as she'd already said in her speech, and her relatives were at the moment flying out to Aceh.

No, her father hadn't been found yet, but the marines were still looking and she was certain he would soon be. No, that wasn't an irrational hope, her father was strong, a survivor, and next question please?

Yes, the remains of her mother had been retrieved from Tiger Island. Yes, yes, yes, she had buried her mother on the beach, hadn't they listened to her speech?

How did she feel about burying her own mother? Well, God, she said, how do you think I felt? But she knew that her anger at the question was a clever sham.

Still the journalists weren't sated. They wanted to devour her with their questions. Sarah glanced out the window, wishing to be outside and alone, and saw several refugee children peering through the louvered panes. A resilient curiosity was back in their eyes.

Another, more genuine anger rose in her. "Why are you all so interested in me?" she said. "We just happened to be passing by. This isn't my tragedy, the Bedford family tragedy. This is an Aceh tragedy. See these kids out there? You should be telling the world their stories, not mine."

She got up, refusing to answer any more questions.

From the back of the room came a familiar voice. "Sarah! Sarah!"

She paused, standing on her toes and squinting

over the crowd. Ruslan pushed forward, leading a man by the hand. She recognized the man at once. Ruslan's father, his smile full of dazed joy. "Thank you, Sarah," he said. "Thank you, thank you."

Sarah started to take his offered hand between both of hers in the polite local way, but then, on an impulse she couldn't stop any more than she could stop the tears blurring her vision, she flung her arms around him as cameras whirred and clicked.

Chapter 29

Ruslan and Sarah rode in the back of a military truck heading for Ujung Karang. He had asked for a lift because Sarah wanted to see his house, which by God's grace and strong construction had not been flattened by the tsunami. His father was at the mayor's office, registering Ruslan's name on the survivor's roll, and couldn't come.

Sarah kept toying with a gold ring on a chain hanging around her neck. "My mother's wedding ring," she said. She bit her lip and released it. "The journalists asked what it was like to bury my own mother. What could I tell them? It was just hard work. I can't feel anything for her. Except, you know, this blank nothing. I know she didn't really love me like she did Peter, but she was my mother. She did her best, I know. Why can't I feel? Am I a monster?"

Ruslan firmly shook his head. "No. Don't you think that."

"It scares me, makes me wonder what kind of person I am."

"You don't have to worry about that, Sarah. I know because I know you."

She gave him a quick smile but said nothing.

The truck drove down the main boulevard, the only street that had been cleared, and stopped by the town's stadium. Ruslan helped Sarah down from the back of the truck and led her across dried mud to his house.

"I couldn't believe it when I first saw it," he said. Even now, on his second visit, there was something shocking about the building's naked appearance, standing alone amidst the ruins of the neighborhood. "What's funny is I ran and ran from the tsunami and nearly drowned anyway, but if I'd just climbed to the roof, I would have been okay."

"But you didn't know."

"No, I didn't." He looked out over the distant point. A half-dozen people picked through the remains of their homes. "So many people didn't know anything."

"Can I look inside?"

"Sure. But everything's ruined."

"Who cares, when you have your father back?"

He didn't have to reply. The house was nothing, less than nothing, not even in the same universe, compared to that.

"I'm so happy for you, Ruslan."

He heard the truth of that in her voice, and saw it too, her happiness rising in her wide smile and in her blue eyes, and this when she still had her own father missing.

"You'll find him," he said. "They might have found him already. You sure you don't want to go back to the boat?"

"No." She took his hand, her long fingers curling around his, the warmth of her soft palm spreading all through him. She held his hand for three heartbeats, four, and then squeezed and let go. "I want to have a look inside."

A foot of drying black mud covered the floor of the front parlor, and the walls and ceiling were badly discolored. A strong mildew odor rose from the damp sofa. Magazines and books lay scattered about, their pages pasted together. The only undamaged item, on the coffee table, was the notebook from the helicopter, opened to the drawing of his father.

She glanced at it and blurted, "But what if my dad's dead?"

How he wished he could give her some of his own father to reassure her. "Don't give up hope, Sarah."

"It's getting to be like this washing machine. Hope, dread, hope, dread. It's about all I can feel."

"That's how I felt too."

She gave him a smile. "You're right. Don't give up hope. Ever. Hey, where's your room?"

"Upstairs."

She climbed the stairs ahead of him. The doors to the three rooms on the second floor were closed. At the top landing she said, "You stay here. I want to guess which room is yours." She walked down the short hall and stopped in front of the third door. "This is your room. Has the best light for drawing and painting."

He grinned. "That's right."

She opened the door.

He belatedly realized something and rushed to intercept her, but he was too late. She'd spotted his drawing of her, still taped to the wall, tinted brown by the water, but the smudged blue of her eyes and pink of her lips still visible. She stood before it, her head tilted a little as she studied it.

He wanted to vanish. "Um, that was when you first stopped in Meulaboh, when your boat engine was broken. I'd never drawn a Westerner."

"It's really . . . do I really look like that?"

Disappointment shot through his embarrassment. "You don't like it?"

"No, no, I like it a lot, but you've made me, I don't know, more mysterious than I am."

"You were mysterious. I didn't know you."

"You made me prettier, too."

The artist in Ruslan said with sure confidence, "That's you, just as you are."

She nodded at the poster of Siti Nurhaliza. "Am I prettier than her?"

Ruslan was about to gallantly say yes, when he paused. His blood sloshed back and forth, and he knew that truth was far more important than flattery.

"No. But she's not you."

Sarah turned to him. He was afraid she could hear his pounding heart. She slipped into his arms, pressed her head against his shoulder. "I don't think Peter and me would've made it if it hadn't been for you," she said. "Thank you."

"You're welcome." What a silly thing to say. Couldn't she feel the way his heart was stampeding all over the place?

She drew away a little to look at him. "Anybody ever tell you that you have beautiful eyes?" she murmured.

He kissed her then. How could he not? It was as easy as falling.

When they finally broke apart, she rested her forehead against his. "You remember what my dad looked like?"

"His nose was a little *bengkok*, bended, to the right. This way." Ruslan pressed a finger to his own nose.

She drew back and smiled. "Broke it in college. An amateur boxing match. He always said he'd get it fixed, but my mom said, don't you dare, I love your nose." Her smile became a laugh. "He'd say, you love me for my nose? and she'd say, absolutely, I fell in love with your nose and I married your nose, and if you change it, I'm going to have to divorce it. You know, a lot of my friends' parents divorced, but I was lucky, I really was." Her laughter died. "Do you think you can draw a picture of him? For good luck, like with your father."

Instead of using the notebook downstairs, he picked up the sketch pad on his desk, the top page already dry from the sunlight, and began to draw.

• • •

Sarah leaned against the windowsill, watching him. She'd be leaving him soon, she knew. They could make promises about staying in touch and all that, but life didn't work that way. Soon, all he'd be was a memory. She wanted to remember this moment for the rest of her life. How he looked. His mussed-up hair. The way the corner of his lips twisted in concentration. The focused look of those gorgeous eyes.

Ruslan remembered to the last wrinkle the face of Sarah's father. But an artist draws the truth of what he sees. And now, after the tsunami, he was seeing more clearly than he had ever seen before. The truth that he needed to distill, for Sarah's sake, guided his hand.

It didn't take long. He had never created anything more true and certain in his life.

Sarah took the sketch that he quietly handed to her.

"Thanks," she said, and then lost all her words. The sketch wasn't of her father.

It was her mother.

And in the simple, graceful lines of her gently smiling face, in the eyes that looked right into her, Sarah saw all the love that her mother had always had for her, and how absolutely, utterly wrong she'd been to have ever doubted it.

Something gave way within her, and the raw waters of grief came rushing in.

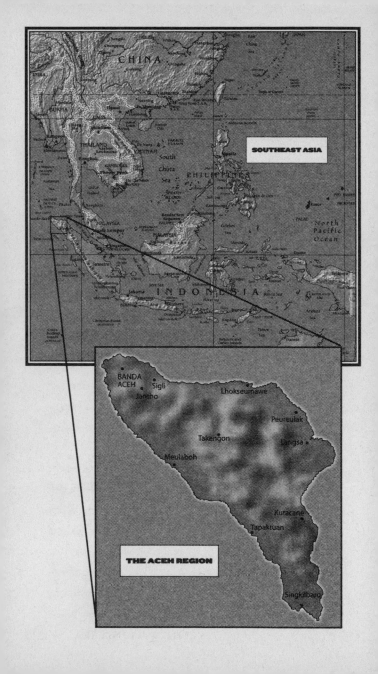

Author's Note

December 26, 2004, dawned bright over the calm Indian Ocean. At 7:59 a.m. local time, deep in the sunless depths one hundred miles off the west coast of Sumatra, an ocean bed fault ruptured for hundreds of miles. An area of seafloor the size of California sprang up as much as twenty-five feet, shoving upward several dozen cubic miles of ocean.

This created a powerful series of waves that in the deep ocean traveled as fast as a jet plane, barely disturbing the surface with their two-foot ripples. When the wave train reached coastal areas, it slowed down. With all that volume of displaced water racing into increasingly shallow water, some of the waves grew to enormous size. Aceh, in northern Indonesia, was the first landmass to be hit, approximately twenty minutes after the quake; it was estimated that the tallest of the waves that struck was a hundred feet high. The waves roared ashore at twenty to thirty miles an hour with enough force to level buildings and destroy fields up to two and a half miles inland.

An Acehnese fisherman one mile out at sea described driving his boat up the steep face of one of these monster waves, already taller than a coconut tree. The fisherman said when the boat finally crested the wave, there was no back side. The top was flat and wide, the wave a huge block of water rushing shoreward with such speed that it generated its own wind, spinning up thick mist.

The wave train reached Thailand about two hours later. As with Aceh, the leading trough of the wave train arrived first. The sea began to drain away from the shore, exposing reef and seabed for up to hundreds of feet. At other places the wave crest was the first to arrive as a giant surge of water. Eleven hours after the earthquake, the tsunami still had power to take lives in South Africa, five thousand miles away from the epicenter. Pouring through continental gaps, the tsunami finally lapped gently ashore in places as far away as Brazil and Nova Scotia.

The wave train battered coastlines for several hours, striking and withdrawing, with up to thirty minutes between crests. Receding waves carried people and debris miles out to sea.

The waves had different characteristics in different areas, depending on local topography. Several Acehnese fishermen anchored off deepwater reefs that nearly drained dry described the biggest wave as a gentle upwelling followed by violent currents. In Thailand, as captured in amateur video footage, the waves broke well offshore into churning white water that swept inland. In west Aceh survivors described the biggest second wave storming ashore on the back of the much smaller first wave like a rearing snake ready to strike them. Eyewitnesses said that when the crest finally toppled well inland, it did so with enough force to gouge trenches into the earth. They described the waves as black—their energy would have stirred up the dark volcanic sand on the coastline's seafloor.

With no warning system in place, the coastal residents and visitors in more than a dozen countries were caught unawares. The tsunami was the deadliest in history, killing nearly a quarter of a million people and leaving over a million homeless. The majority of fatalities and the greatest destruction occurred in Aceh.

I have been to Aceh several times over the years, and spent a month as a volunteer relief aide worker in western Aceh in the immediate aftermath of the tsunami. While I draw on that experience and on countless conversations with survivors and refugees, and have tried to be accurate about the details of the quake and the ensuing tsunami based on survivors' accounts, it should be kept in mind that this is a work of fiction and not journalism. Tiger Island is a composite of several Acehnese islands, although the island's small herd of wild elephants, which are found on the Sumatran mainland, is strictly an author's imaginative touch. Meulaboh and Calang are real towns that were devastated by the tsunami, but for purposes of the story, I have rearranged somewhat the topography between them and altered some minor details. The novel's community of survivors at Calang is fictional but draws on actual events in other towns. For the sake of narrative, I have also shortened the time between the tsunami and the first significant arrival of aid.

The need in Aceh remains great. Despite generous giving, many families are still quietly, almost invisibly, suffering. I am donating a portion of my royalties from this book to one or two local organizations working at a grassroots level to help the Acehnese people.

Here's a look at
RICHARD LEWIS's next novel:

The Demon Queen

JESSE ALWAYS SAT IN CORNERS. For one thing, corners were often the safest place to be. Nobody could creep up behind him. He also learned a lot just sitting there and watching, although some people didn't like it when he did. When he was six or seven, one of his foster mothers, who drank six-packs of beer for her lunches, stomped over to the nook where he was sitting and walloped him over the head. "Stop looking at me like that," she said.

This morning, Jesse sat at his usual desk in the back of his ninth-grade home room at Prairie Progressive. The other students settled into their seats, chattering about their plans for the coming weekend, ignoring him. They were all midwestern white, and he was . . . well, he didn't know what he was, exactly, except he wasn't white and he sure wasn't midwestern. He had skin the color of weak tea, high cheekbones that could have been copied from an Aztec carving, round black eyes like an Asian, and black curly hair tinted with reddish streaks, as though it had been singed by fire. But this wasn't why they ignored him. After all, the popular star running back on the football team was one of the several Hispanics in the school, and the student body vice president was an Asian American. No, it was simply that Jesse was not only the newest student, but he was also from California, which was not just out of state but another country altogether.

Jesse stared out the window at the churning, tumbling clouds. He'd spent most of his life in Los Angeles, and he wasn't used to this prairie weather. Two months in Longview with his latest foster parents and he'd already found out the sky here had a temper like one of those wild elephants on *National Geographic*. Big and slow and then bam, it was charging down on you. The local weatherman had said the weather was going to be fine. Fine for a tornado, maybe. The way the light was fighting with the shadows, with clouds zooming in to close a patch of sun and a ray bursting out from another spot, it seemed as though some cosmic battle was going on. The trees closest to the window shook in the wind, but on the other side of the street, the trees were still.

"All right, everybody, let's quiet down," Mrs. Bender said. "I have some announcements."

As usual, nobody paid attention. It took Mrs. Bender several hollers at increasing volume to get everybody to shut up.

The classroom door opened. Jesse turned to look. A tanned blond girl stood to the side of the doorway, glancing into the room. She had thick glasses and clunky earrings. Her books were stuffed into a basket of woven reeds.

"Excuse me," she said.

Mrs. Bender looked up from the papers on her desk. "Ah, there you are."

"I went down the other hall."

"Never mind, you're here." Mrs. Bender waved her in.

The room fell silent as the girl entered. Betsy Keelan whispered, "God. Fashion disaster."

Jesse didn't see anything wrong with her clothes. Half the girls in the class were wearing jeans, and as for the girl's red blouse, it had all the right curves in the right places. She stood by Mrs. Bender's desk, looking down at her strapped sandals.

Mrs. Bender stood. "Everybody, this is Honor Clarke. A new student. Her parents have just arrived from China and so she's joining us late." She smiled at the girl. "Honor, why don't you tell us something about yourself?"

Honor glanced up at Mrs. Bender. "Not China. Bali. That's in Indonesia. My dad was killed. That's why we're late." She had a slight accent, each word fully enunciated, the consonants crisply pronounced.

"Oh my, I didn't know," Mrs. Bender said. "I'm so sorry to hear that."

Andy Turnbull straightened his thick shoulders "Indonesia? Did terrorists blow him up or something?"

Mrs. Blender gave him a warning look. "Why don't you just take a seat, Honor?"

Honor ignored her. With her forefinger, she pushed her glasses up her nose and blinked at Andy. "Actually, people said black magic. We got his body back but not his head."

Jesse jerked upright. The wall clock's tick-tick-tick swelled to fill the silence.

Mrs. Bender took a deep breath to say something, but Honor rode right over her. "My mom's an anthropologist who studies witchcraft and black magic and the Bali police thought she might have done it, so that's why they held her and why we're late. Any more questions?"

There weren't any. Mrs. Bender gestured toward the desks. "We're happy to have you, dear."

Honor walked to the back, twenty pairs of eyes following her. Out of the three empty desks, she picked the one next to Jesse. Sitting sideways on her chair, she put down her basket and took off her glasses to clean them on the hem of her blouse.

Jesse squinted at her earrings. Were those *scorpions*? They were scorpions, all right, little ones frozen in plastic cubes with their stingers raised. And frozen in the plastic bracelet around her wrist was a long black centipede with yellow legs and a big red head.

She put on her glasses and looked at him. Her eyes were gray, the color of thin ice over dark water. After a slight hesitation, he wriggled his fingers in welcome. It was the least he could do, now that he wasn't the newest student in the school. "Hi," he whispered.

Her eyes widened in sudden alarm. She shrank back a little and hissed words under her breath that he didn't understand, something urgent and challenging, almost hostile.

"What?" he said, more confused than offended by her reaction.

She stared at him for a moment longer, her alarm fading, and then straightened in her chair.

He lowered his hand. "Fine, then," he muttered.

Yet there was a little itch in the back of his mind. It wasn't just her odd reaction. He'd never seen her before in his life. But it was as though he knew this girl from somewhere.

About the Author

Richard Lewis is the son of American missionary parents. Although he attended a university in the United States, he was born and raised and now lives in Bali, Indonesia. He volunteered in Aceh after the tsunami of 2004 and witnessed firsthand the turmoil following the natural disaster. Visit his website at www.richardlewisauthor.com.

A note from Richard Lewis:

"The need in Aceh remains great. Despite generous giving, many families are still quietly, almost invisibly, suffering. I am donating a portion of my royalties from this book to one or two local organizations working at a grassroots level to help the Acehnese people."

GARY PAULSEN
Three-time Newbery Honor author

Newbery Honor Book   Newbery Honor Book

From Simon Pulse • Published by Simon & Schuster

AMANDA MARRONE

LISA McMANN

MOVE OUTSIDE THE REALM OF NORMAL

WITH THESE DANGEROUSLY GOOD BOOKS.

KRISTOPHER REISZ

LISA SCHROEDER

UGLIES
SCOTT WESTERFELD

READ THE BRAIN-KICKING
NEW YORK TIMES **BESTSELLERS:**

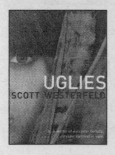  

AND DON'T MISS THE FOURTH BOOK:

PUBLISHED BY SIMON PULSE